Advance Praise for KNEE DEEP

"*Knee Deep* is a love letter to New Orleans that is written for young adults and new adults but will tug at the heartstrings of readers of all ages."

— Medium.com

"I don't even know where to start with describing the pure beauty of this book. It was exactly what I needed to read at this moment in time."

— A Quintillion Words

"Hoeffner takes the gumbo of New Orleans' people and culture and mixes them into something wonderfully unexpected."

-David Clawson, author of *My Fairy Godmother is a Drag Queen*

" This is a coming of age book, which deals with first love, loss and a little bit of voodoo thrown in. I got quickly lost in the book and kept turning the pages…a great read."

— The Book Lover's Bouidor

"This is worth the read for the descriptions about Mardi Gras alone."

— Nothing But Room

KNEE DEEP

Karol Hoeffner

Fitzroy Books

Published by Fitzroy Books
An imprint of
Regal House Publishing, LLC
Raleigh, NC 27612
All rights reserved

https://fitzroybooks.com

Printed in the United States of America

ISBN -13 (paperback): 9781646030095
ISBN -13 (hardcover): 9781646030507
ISBN -13 (epub): 9781646030361
Library of Congress Control Number: 2020930409

Interior and cover design by Lafayette & Greene
lafayetteandgreene.com
Cover images © by C.B. Royal

Regal House Publishing, LLC
https://regalhousepublishing.com

Printed in the United States of America

This book is dedicated to everyone who has ever:

Caught beads at a Mardi Gras parade,
Eaten a soft-shell crab po-boy at Jazz Fest,
Yelled "Who Dat?" in the high seats of the Superdome,
Danced all the way through Twelfth Night,
Crossed that bridge over Lake Pontchartrain in search of boudin sausage,
Or fallen in love in Congo Square.

And to those poor souls who have done none of these things,
Swear to yourself to do at least one.

1.

Y ou know how people are always saying, "What happens in Vegas stays in Vegas"? Well, what happens in New Orleans mainly gets ignored. The truly bizarre might end up as the punch line in a joke, but nobody gets their panties in a twist over comings and goings that ain't any of their business. Let me explain what I mean. I once saw a little man, no more than three feet tall, dressed in a tuxedo chasing after a naked lady down Bourbon Street and nobody around me even blinked an eye.

I did not have a regular childhood.

I spent my formative years doing my homework bellied up to my daddy's bar, a seedy-looking establishment in the shadow of Bourbon Street. And even though bartending is a highly respected occupation in New Orleans, I hated telling my friends what he did for a living, not because I was ashamed, but because that question was always followed by asking where he worked. You see, my issue wasn't with his running a bar; it was the name of the bar itself that was the problem.

The Cock's Comb.

Try explaining to teenage boys with nothing but sex and dirt on their mind, that cock's comb refers to the fleshy red skin on top of a rooster's head. It does not work; I was the butt of many jokes. And did I mention that I hate being teased?

Two summers ago, when I left an all-girls middle school for a co-ed Catholic high school, St. Bede the Venerable in the Ninth Ward, I begged Daddy to change the bar's name to something less objectionable like Camille's (my given name) Bar and Grill.

"Now, sweetie, you know I would do anything for you," he'd

told me, "but the Cock's Comb has been in our family since my daddy's daddy won it in a poker game from a gambler off the riverboat. These walls breathe history. Jean Lafitte sold his stolen goods in the back room. And Lee Harvey Oswald sat in that corner booth all by himself and ordered up a White Russian. The name of this bar and all it implies gives meaning to our lives. Sweetie, we are nothing without a sense of place."

He was right about that. Where we live defines who we are. I spent so much time living in that bar, watching the clientele change as the sun moved across the sky. The afternoons were reserved for media types, journalists, and a few fiction writers who were replaced in early evening by what my mother called the "ne'er-do-wells" and what my daddy argued were "the true citizens of 'Orleans." And late nights, the tattooed and pierced stumbled in. I grew up telling time by who pushed open the massive oak door and walked inside.

But none of us—not my parents, nor my cross-dressing tutor, nor either of my best friends—could have predicted the evil that would push through the doors of our lives following the tragedy of summer. Our story is a tale of survival, of those who lived and those who died. And although it is *our* story, I will begin with me because I am the one telling it.

All my life, I've been called a "Mardi Gras baby," because, according to my daddy, I was conceived on Twelfth Night, which marks the day that the Three Kings came to Bethlehem to see the Baby Jesus. And as everyone within shouting distance of New Orleans knows, the Mardi Gras season of parades and parties begins with Twelfth Night and ends with the biggest street party of all on Fat Tuesday. Evidently, it was also the beginning of me.

I was conceived by parents who really weren't ready to have a kid. It wasn't that they were too young. My father, Donald Darveau, was almost forty and my mother, Mary Ellen Price, was a very mature twenty-five. They met right after she graduated from Southern Methodist University with a degree in economics. A job waited for her at a Houston investment firm but before she joined the rank and file of the executive class, she wanted one last fling in party city. So, she came to New Orleans for Jazz Fest.

The night before she met my dad, my mother stayed up all night drinking Long Island iced teas and listening to Dr. John sing "Gris-Gris Gumbo Ya, Tipitina." The next morning, she made a mad dash across Jackson Square to join a Second Line parade coming out of the St. Louis Cathedral. Hung over and blurry-eyed, she ran into my father who, quite literally, knocked her off her feet.

He liked to say, "The day I met your mother was like finding a bird's nest on the ground."

Being a true Southern gentleman, he helped her up, brushed her off, and whisked her away to the Cock's Comb so that she could recover. There, in the empty bar—all the regulars were at the Fair Grounds for Jazz Fest—he mixed up one of his famous Bloody Marys, poured it into a tall glass, served it alongside a basket of crab-stuffed Jalapeno hushpuppies, and asked her if she believed in love at first sight.

"I am not a romantic person," Mary Ellen answered.

"I disagree," he said. "Only a romantic person would follow a total stranger into an empty bar in the middle of the Quarter."

"Or a fool," she replied, taking her first sip of what she later called the best Bloody Mary in the history of the world.

"And you clearly are no fool," my daddy said.

She took another long sip of her drink and listened to him describe the colorful history of his bar and the people who frequented it. "Many from the other side."

"Other side of what?" Mary Ellen wondered and hazarded a guess. "Lake Pontchartrain?"

"No, I was referring to what lies beyond the life we know. New Orleans is peopled with souls tethered to the Crescent City and unable to move on to the sweet hereafter for one reason or another. Pirates, Voodoo Queens, Kings of Carnival—they all like to hang out at my bar," he added with a wink.

My mother, who did not believe in ghosts or love at first sight, had the distinct impression they were not alone.

Like my daddy, I was convinced that there was a thin line between life and death. But where he counted ghostly visitations to his bar as evidence, I saw visions of the afterlife at sunset, on the horizon where sky meets water. Sometimes, even now, when I stand on the riverbank in the hazy glow between day and night, I feel the presence of others, as if I could actually reach out and touch the recently departed. Oh, but I'm getting way ahead of myself—again.

Back to the oft-repeated story of my conception. My parents had been seeing each other for some time when he invited her to a Twelfth Night party in the Garden District. After a couple of drinks, they slipped away unnoticed to a guest bedroom at the far end of the house. Back in the dining room, a gathering costumed crowd of harlequins, pirates, and jesters were admiring a glorious King's cake sprinkled with granulated sugar tinted purple, green, and gold, the colors of Carnival. Baked inside the rich batter was a tiny ceramic baby doll and, according to tradition, whoever got the piece of cake with the baby in it had to throw the next party. Everyone in the room was having a gay old time, talking and laughing and drinking, when a six-foot-plus buccaneer eagerly accepted a slice of the cake, bit down on the tiny ceramic baby, broke her molar on its pointy little head, and screamed bloody murder.

Down the hall, my mother also screamed when my father explained what else had broken—his Deluxe Trojan condom. Those were, thankfully, the only two casualties of that Twelfth Night. But quite frankly, my mother would have preferred to have broken her tooth on a ceramic baby than to have conceived a real one.

Now it may seem strange to you that I know so much about my own conception, but the sad truth is my parents are always either having sex or talking about it, which I find equally annoying. And the sadder truth is that my parents did not need a baby to make their life complete. Now, I don't want you to think that they don't love me, because they do, but the simple fact of the matter is that all they have ever needed or wanted was each other.

My entire life I have felt like an extra bracelet on the arm of an overly accessorized drag queen.

And that is why my two best friends—Gina, pronounced with a long *I* as in va-gina, who lives in a mansion in the Garden District and acts slutty to offset her social pedigree; and Beano Benoit, the only gay quarterback on the varsity football team whose love for the game is equally matched by his talent for musical theater—believe that there is not a romantic bone in my body. They are convinced that the reason I have never had a serious boyfriend is because of the romantic drama I have had to endure in the form of my parents' marriage.

But they are wrong. Terribly, terribly wrong. Every time I walk through the Quarter and look up at the shuttered windows and wrought-iron balconies, I feel the lusty emotions that linger from all who have lived there before. I hear love stories in the steamy jazz that floats out of bars and in the Second Line parades that jam narrow cobblestone streets. For heavens' sake, the very first bus I rode when I was little was named Desire. That right there tells you something, explains how I grew up different, how the very act of living in New Orleans meant that romance was in my DNA, no matter what my best friends thought.

Of course, they had no idea that I was obsessing over someone, because I managed to keep the object of my own desire a secret from everybody, including and especially those two. I was pretty sure they would disapprove of my loving him, so I kept my silence. But in the middle of that hot, steamy summer and with August approaching, I was almost ready to say his name out loud.

2.

One thing for sure—if it's August in New Orleans, it's gonna be crazy hot. A week before my sixteenth birthday on one of those drippy, sweaty, so-muggy-you-can-barely-breathe kind of evenings, Beano, Gina, and I sat out on my front porch. We were swatting bugs with bible verse paper fans that Beano scored three weeks before at a church rummage sale in Lakeshore and sipping iced tea. Gina wanted to escape inside to air-conditioned comfort, but Beano could not be coaxed into the cool house; he lived for sweltering summer nights and acted like *hot as hell* was a gift from God.

"Humidity is sexy," Beano argued.

A Tennessee Williams fan, Beano consciously fashioned himself after the Maggie character in *Cat on a Hot Tin Roof*, who spent most of her time running around in her white satin slip, wiping the sweat off her chest and making lusty, sensual advances toward her pathetic husband.

Just so you know, that was Beano to a *T*.

"What are we gonna do about my birthday this year? It's only a week away."

"Why not do a Disney princess theme party, only make it nasty," Beano suggested.

"Do not ruin Camille's special day just because you have a secret desire to dress up like Arial in a padded seashell bra," Gina said.

"Number one, a seashell bra does not require padding. And number two, if we're doing the nasty princess thing, I'm in for Mulan," Beano said.

"Of all the princesses, Mulan is the least likely to do the nasty," Gina said.

"True, but I would look fabulous in a kimono," Beano shot back, posing theatrically.

Gina turned to me. "Seriously, Camille, you could invite a bunch of lame kids from school to your house for an even lamer dance-slash-barbecue, or we could go to the Quarter and have a real party because I know this guy who knows this guy." Gina's voice trailed off as she envisioned an evening of planned debauchery. When illegal substances were required, Gina always knew a guy who knew a guy who was only too happy to oblige.

Don't get me wrong. I love the Quarter. But I had something else in mind. "I know it's late notice and all, but can we do a party at your house?" I asked Gina.

Gina lived on St. Charles Street in the lush Garden District in a mansion built in a style Gina's mother described as "a modified French château." As impressed as I was with the house's architectural pedigree and the fact that Gina had a four-room suite for a bedroom, what really wowed me was the backyard. The entire back of Gina's house opened up to a formal French parterre garden, complete with ornate fountains and water works divided by beds of clipped boxwoods, herbs, and roses. At night, especially in the summer, Gina's garden was possibly the most romantic place in all of New Orleans: the perfect setting for what I had in mind.

"What you people doin' outside? Air-conditioning break or something?"

I looked up and saw my next-door neighbor, eighteen-year-old Antwone Despre, walking up the sidewalk with swag, home from his two-a-day football practice, helmet in hand. Reaching the front porch, he leaned against the Corinthian-style pillar, wiped the sweat from his brow, and asked Beano, "Why weren't you at practice, bro?"

Beano's voice dropped an octave. "Groin pull," he said, punctuating his two-word excuse with a macho cough.

"Got any more of that tea?" Antwone asked, brightening the dusk with his languid smile.

"I'll get you a glass," Beano said, eager to avoid further conversation regarding ditching practice.

"Sweet tea's on the first shelf in the fridge," I hollered at Beano as he left to fetch it.

We always kept two kinds of tea in the house, sweetened and unsweetened. My mother, not being a true Southerner—people who say Texas is part of the South are just plain uninformed—preferred Lipton without sugar or lemon. But Antwone, like most of New Orleans, liked his tea sweet. I took a moment to admire him in the gathering darkness, hoping that the twilight would hide my deep appreciation. He was a light-skinned Black man with eyes as green as the reeds sprouting on the banks of the mighty Mississippi. And don't get me started on his body, which could be compared to a Greek god, a real live Adonis. Well, you get the picture.

I have known Antwone all my life. He and his grandmother—whom everyone calls Bama, short for her given name Alabama Birmingham—lived next-door in a shotgun house identical to my own, only with the floor plan flipped. My bedroom was on the west side of the house; his bedroom on the east. Our houses were so close together we could listen in on each other's lives.

I've looked up to Antwone since I was five, but I remember quite clearly the moment I fell in love with him. It was on a Wednesday in the late afternoon in March when I was fourteen. I was on my way home from basketball practice. Even though I was short and a girl, I played point guard on a boys' team. (I have since given up the sport.) Eddie Deville, a smart-ass bench warmer, followed me home, screaming insults like "Ball-hog" and "Poser" and "Our fat forward's got bigger tits than you."

I knew that he was pissed because I was on the court and he was not, but after a while, his teasing began to wear me down. I made a sharp turn onto my street and sprinted toward my front porch, flying up the steps like I was going in for a layup. But as I reached the door, he called out the final insult. "Your momma must have slept with someone 'sides your daddy, 'cause you got hair like Ben Wallace."

And that was when I burst into tears.

In case you don't know, Ben Wallace was the most kick-ass small forward to ever play basketball, but he also had the worst hair in the entire history of the NBA, the wildest mess you have ever seen on or off a court.

My own hair has been a source of contention all my life. It's impossibly thick, coarse, and wiry. My mother has straight-as-a-board, silky, fine hair and not a clue as to what to do with mine. She's tried frying my scalp with chemicals; she's burned my hair with the same iron she uses to press my daddy's shirts. As a last resort, she finally grabbed me up on a Saturday morning and the two of us took the streetcar to a Black beauty shop downtown. It was there, at the Salon Baptiste on Chartres Street, I found my salvation.

I was ushered to the back of the salon and introduced to its owner, Aisha, who was the most elegant lady I'd ever laid eyes on. She cooed at me with a voice that dripped molasses. "Excuse me for staring, but it's been a long time since I've seen a nappy-headed white girl. Sit down in this chair and let me take a closer look at you."

"I'm sorry it's such a mess. But I can't even get a comb through it," my mother said as Aisha circled the chair, studying my hair.

"It may be a mess now, but I see a head full of possibility. I love the color. Why, it's like spun gold. My word, child, do you know how special you are?"

I leaned back into the chair, letting her words resonate. All my life, people had talked about my hair as if it were some kind of problem that needed to be solved, and now here was this beautiful angel of a woman telling me that my hair was *like spun gold*. Those three little words raised my self-esteem by about a hundred points.

Aisha was almost six feet tall; her limbs were long and lean. She moved like a gazelle and her arms looked like they could stretch around the world. She ran her pencil-thin fingers through my hair, which became more manageable under her steady hand. After examining the texture and length, she suggested braiding my hair. She said it would flatter the shape of my face as well as being practical since, with gentle washing, the *'do* could last over a month. Mary Ellen was all over that like white on rice.

"You wanna go and do some errands because this could take a while?" Aisha asked my mother, hand on her slim hip.

Mary Ellen smiled and with a flip of her hand, said, "Oh, I'll stay. I don't mind," thinking it would take one hour, tops, to braid a kid's hair.

Three hours later, Aisha was still working her magic, weaving my hair in and out with an underhand, upward motion. She reminded me of a symphony conductor, orchestrating my hair into a melodic piece of organization, tight little braids close to my scalp in rows as straight as planted corn. And at the end of each row, she buttoned the braid with a cowry shell that came all the way from the Ivory Coast of Africa.

Meanwhile, my mother was bored to tears. She fidgeted on the chintz print sofa, watching the steady parade of clients who came through the door, most of whom stayed longer than me.

"You can leave if you want, Mary Ellen. I'll be okay," I said.

"Whatcha doin' calling your momma by her given name?" Aisha demanded, alarmed by my lack of propriety.

"She started when she was little. We think because that's what my husband called me," Mary Ellen explained. "At first we thought it was cute. So, she kept doing it."

"Well, I think it's disrespectful." Aisha did not mince words. "What do you call your daddy?"

"Daddy," I answered.

"Well, at least there's that," Aisha said.

After our first visit, Mary Ellen just dropped me off at the Salon Baptiste, which suited Aisha and me just fine. And as I waited my turn, I watched the comings and goings of Black women from behind my *Ebony Magazine*. And gradually, I was accepted into this sorority of women and girls of all ages. It didn't matter that I was white and they were Black; we came together as sisters of the comb, united in our mutual dislike of nappiness. We crowded into the shop the way office workers gather around the water cooler to discuss the way the world turned. The place was alive with knowledge, bristling with stories, and teeming with wisdom. Getting your hair done at the Salon Baptiste was often an all-day affair and I got more than cornrow braids; I received an education.

"The three most important things in life are God, family, and hair," Aisha told me one day as she buttoned my braids with bright colored beads. "Child, do you know anything about the African Diaspora?"

I did not, so she explained that it was the story of how her people, torn away their from home in Africa, managed to hold on to the links to their past lives as they formed a whole new culture.

"My great-grandmother, who lived to be a 106, told me that our people have always known that the head is the highest spiritual part of the body, which is why we are very particular about who lays their hands on our heads."

I, too, became very particular about who laid hands on my head, which is why I got into it with Eddie. The week before, I had put off my regular appointment at the Salon Baptiste because Aisha was on vacation in Florida visiting her sister. And since I would not let anybody else but her touch my hair, I had to manage it myself until she got back. I unbraided my cornrows, washed my hair, and pulled it back into a cockeyed ponytail.

By the time I ran home after practice, my hair was a royal mess. Truth be told, I probably did look a lot like Ben Wallace.

But Eddie's words—flung from just a few feet away—inflamed old insecurities. I was not just plain old mad but burning, crazy mad, the kind that can land you in jail.

I scrambled down the porch and attacked my teammate head-on, swinging my fists wildly at his chest. I was more fit than he was so I should have had some sort of advantage. But he outweighed me by twenty pounds. Plus, although I had him on mad, he had me on mean. And mean wins over mad every time.

He pounced on me like one of those hulking giants from the WWF; he straddled his legs across my chest and pinned my arms to the ground. I couldn't move. I could barely breathe. I envisioned a thousand scenarios, all of which would end up with me in the hospital.

But what he did do was worse than anything I could imagine, an unspeakable, unconscionable act.

He spit on my hair.

As his disgusting mouth juice ran down my curls and onto my cheek, I clenched my eyes shut so that he could not see how small and dirty he made me feel. My eyes closed, fighting back tears, I heard a bus roaring down our street. The brakes squealed as it stopped right in front of my house. I knew it was the late bus from high school, the one that carried the sixth-period athletes home, and the thought of all those faces pressed to the window to witness my utter humiliation made me want to throw up.

Not about to give in, I kicked him hard in the groin and pushed him off me in one swift, unexpected movement. I scrambled to my feet and stood tall as Eddie curled up in pain. He took a deep breath, jumped to his feet, and lunged at me with murder in his eyes. But he was stopped cold a split second before he made contact.

"What's the fuss?" Antwone asked, holding Eddie back by the scruff of his neck.

At sixteen, Antwone already looked more like a man than a boy with his fine, broad shoulders and whittled waist. In the next two years, he would set district records for yards rushing. But on this day, in my front yard, all he wanted to do was set the record straight.

"What's goin' on here?" Antwone asked, casual as can be.

"She kicked me in the balls," Eddie whined.

"What did you do to her?"

"I was just defending myself," Eddie continued, which I had to admit was only half a lie. "We were walking home from practice, talking shit to each other. Back and forth. You know how it is. And then all of a sudden, she goes crazy and comes after me like some crack whore."

"That true?" Antwone turned to me. He was a stickler for being fair and playing by the rules. In his entire football career, he would never be called for a late hit or illegal motion or any of that.

"Well, I did take the first swing," I replied.

Eddie started in again, going on and on about how I might have ruined him for life by kicking his nuts. He said he doubted if he would be able to father children, which in my opinion might be a good thing.

"That's all very fine and well, but you still haven't told me what you DID to set her off."

Eddie shrunk back. "Well, I guess I might have said some stuff I shouldn't have said."

"What kind of stuff?"

I hoped Eddie would man up and apologize. But when he didn't, I jumped right in with the truth.

"Stuff like my daddy wasn't my daddy. That my mother slept with someone else."

"Oh, that's bad," Antwone said, tightening his grip.

"But that wasn't what set me off."

"You mean there's more?"

"Yes, there is," I said, taking a deep, meaningful breath. "HE INSULTED MY HAIR."

A long pause ensued. A very, very long pause. As a man raised among proud Black women, Antwone deeply understood the sanctity of the hair.

"You're lucky she didn't kill you," he said quietly before asking how I wanted to handle the situation. Eddie cowered. The color slowly drained from his face. He knew he didn't stand a chance against Antwone who could whip him easy, one hand tied behind his back. I took a moment to revel in the fact that this big bully had been reduced to a sniveling, scared little piece of shit, and his fate was up to me.

"Let him go," I said in a rare display of mercy.

Before he released him, Antwone got up in his face: "I swear to you, if you ever chase her, bully her, taunt her, tease her, lay a hand on her, or say one thing—good or bad—about her hair, I will hunt you down like the dog you are."

By the time Antwone let him go, Eddie was already gone, hurtling down the street at record speed.

"Thanks," I said, giving Antwone a playful punch on his arm.

He smiled and shrugged. "Damn, you do hit hard for a girl."

"Thanks again," I said and then added, "for, you know, helping me out."

"You don't need anybody to fight your battles. You can rescue yourself, baby girl. That's for sure."

That was the first time he called me "baby girl." I looked into his deep green eyes and felt like I was seeing him for the very first time.

As we walked up to my front porch, my feelings for my childhood friend changed course. I plunged from affection into waters of deep devotion, like a babbling brook that rushes over rocks and spills into a full-fledged river. Looking back, I realize that it wasn't his coming to my defense that made me see him in a different light. It was when he told me that I didn't need him to fight my battles that I fell in love. I could have grabbed him and kissed him and done him right there in the middle of the front yard.

But I didn't.

And I haven't.

Not yet.

Two years later, sitting on my front porch on a sweltering

night, swatting bugs bigger 'n Dallas, I was certain of our final destination—love forever true. Unfortunately, Antwone had not yet bought a ticket on the love train. But when it comes to love, guys can be as dense as water and dumb as dirt.

Beano rejoined us on the porch, carrying a glass of sweet tea, which he handed to Antwone who downed it in one big gulp. And the four of us shot the breeze for about fifteen minutes or so. Antwone was an easy talker; he had a way of making people feel immediately comfortable in their own skin. I guess you could say he brought out the best in folks. I mainly listened, struggling to figure out a way to return the conversation to my birthday party.

"Well, I better go get showered," Antwone said, taking his leave.

"My birthday's Saturday," I blurted out.

"Well, I guess it is," he said, smiling.

"I'm having a party at Gina's house."

"We haven't cleared that yet—" Gina started.

"Starts around seven," I interrupted her.

"Good time for a party."

"That's what I thought," I said, sweating bullets.

"Something you want to ask me, Camille?"

It was time for me to make my first move.

"Wanna come?"

He smiled and brushed my cheek with the back of his hand. "I'll be there, baby girl. And I promise to bring you something special because sixteen should be sweet."

I could have died right then and there and been okay. But while I was luxuriating in the memory of how he sounded when he called me "baby girl," another voice called out from the sidewalk as sharp as a blade.

"What you doin' over there, Antwone?"

His brow furrowed for a fleeting moment. He replaced his frown with his award-winning smile and turned to greet the elusive and cold-as-ice M—, his girlfriend of the hour. Well, actually, they had been going together for over a year, but the fact they had lasted that long was nothing short of a miracle. I personally expected them to break up at any minute. Not that she didn't have plenty to recommend her. M— was six feet tall, almost as tall as he was; her skin was a shade darker and she was drop-dead gorgeous, if you like the model type. Plus, she was smart, a straight-A student, and ambitious. People said she was well-rounded, but I knew better; she had too many sharp edges. Even the way she spelled her first name was irritating. Her given name was Emily and the correct nickname should have been spelled *Em*. Instead, she signed her papers with an M—, which she scripted using too many curlicues followed by a dash. The end result smacked of misplaced self-importance, like she thought she was a diva or something. The girl couldn't even sing.

What bothered me most was that she never appreciated Antwone for who he was; she was always pushing him to do better, to be better. Now, if you must know and haven't already figured out, I hated that girl almost as much as I loved Antwone.

"You're early?" Antwone said as she approached with a studied sashay to her hips.

"No, you're late; you told me to pick you up at seven," M— said, putting a hand on his shoulder and kissing him on the lips in more of a show of ownership than affection. "And sweaty," she added.

"Don't worry. I clean up fast. Give me five and then I'm all yours." Antwone walked back to his house, his arm draped across her shoulder.

"Are they not the most perfect couple?" Beano asked, echoing the sentiment shared by the entire senior class at St. Bede's who had in fact voted Antwone and M— "Most Perfect Couple."

"That is a thoroughly high-school-yearbook way of looking at the world," I said.

"It's classic opposites attract. He's so warm, she's so cold," Beano continued. "Plus, they are both too fabulous-looking.

They should get married, have a ton of kids, and make the world a prettier place."

"She's just using him. And someday he's going to realize that she doesn't love him, at least not the way a woman should love a man."

"What the hell, Camille? I thought you were just crushing on him. But you totally like him," Gina said, her disapproval growing.

"A little, maybe. So what?" I hedged.

"Well, that's just stupid," Gina said.

"Way to be supportive." Beano put his arm around me.

"I'm only saying this because I love you, but liking Antwone Despre is a waste of time," Gina pronounced.

"Why?"

"Because he loves somebody else. Duh and double duh."

"That never stopped you," I pointed out.

"I might hook up with a guy who's in a relationship, but I would never, ever under any circumstances *like* a guy who's already one half of a couple."

"Did you hear the way he called me 'baby girl'?" I asked.

"Guys say stuff like that because they think it makes them sound cool," Beano offered.

Antwone didn't need words to make him sound cool. Like the lone saxophone player who plays on Dauphine Street, rain or shine, Antwone was born cool.

"Good lord, Camille, he calls everybody 'baby girl.' It doesn't mean anything," Gina said, exasperated.

It was unbelievable to me that Gina, with her vast experience, couldn't hear the difference in the way he said those words to me, how his voice transformed into a sugary sweetness. No, there was definitely something special about the way he called me "baby girl." Gina was right about so many things, but when she missed the mark, she missed by a mile.

3.

Gina's words of caution weighed heavy on me. What if she was right? Worried that I might easily blow my one big chance to make Antwone see me in a more favorable romantic light, I decided I might need some help. So on a rainy afternoon, I wandered into the Bone Lady Voodoo Shop on Decatur. The owner, Miss Fleurette, was a prominent and well-respected root queen. Word on the street was that her lineage went all the way back to High Priestess Marie Laveau, the most famous voodoo queen of them all.

"Aren't you Donald Darveau's daughter?" Miss Fleurette asked as I entered her store, studying me like I was a map.

I was not surprised that she knew me, since I practically lived in the Quarter.

We chit-chatted awhile about this and that, like where to find the best pecan pralines. And when the conversation came to a pause, she said matter-of-factly: "I assume you are here for a love potion."

"How did you know?"

She just smiled. "The tenor of your voice hinted at your intention. But your aura screamed the truth. It's been a long time since I've seen someone so young so full of unrequited passion. Who is this object of your desire?"

"The boy next door. Literally. And deep down, I believe he loves me. It's just that, well, you know how complicated feelings can be, especially when you're young."

"What you need is a potion that will open his eyes and his heart to his deep-seated feelings for you."

"Bingo."

She disappeared into the back and returned in twenty minutes with a small bottle of liquid purple, the color of a troubled sky before a storm. She handed it to me and told me that before I saw him, I was to light a candle, focus on my intention, and then dab a drop or two of the potion on a pulse point, like the inside of my wrist or behind my ear.

"If that doesn't get immediate results, you come on back because some situations take more work and equipment."

I got the potion and the advice for only fifteen dollars and ninety-nine cents, a bargain at twice the cost. I left the store and disappeared into the crowded streets of the Quarter, convinced that my secret love would not be a secret for much longer.

That night, as the crescent moon inched its way across the inky sky, I was hunkered down in my bed, listening to a jazzy ballad, imagining the moment when I, drenched in love potion, slow-danced with Antwone in Gina's moonlit garden. Suddenly I heard rustling outside the house, followed by the sound of soft voices, as distasteful to me as they were familiar. My bedroom overlooked the stoop next door, where Antwone and M— sometimes made out. Okay, they made out a lot, not that I was listening or anything. Antwone told Beano he never got it on with M— in front of her own house because she was a moaner when she got excited and he did not want her uptight daddy barging out of the house to kick his ass. So they used the porch in the side yard of his own home because his grandma was near deaf and a heavy sleeper.

Unfortunately, his stoop backed up to my bedroom window, making me an unwitting voyeur. On that night, my window drapes were drawn, so my view was thankfully blocked. Still, I didn't want to listen to her sighs and his sweet-talk, so I cranked up the volume on the music and pulled the covers up over my head, even though it was over eighty degrees in my air-conditioned room. But the anger in her voice grew so loud that it penetrated my protective cocoon.

"Don't you touch me. 'Cause I am so not over being mad at you."

I threw off the covers. I didn't want to witness their fooling around, but I sure wasn't going to miss out on an argument. I lived for their disagreements and strained to overhear what appeared to be the beginning of one.

"Why you so upset? When did you ever say no to a party—especially one in the Garden District?" Antwone asked.

"Well, you should have asked me first before you go making promises to that nappy-headed white girl!"

And there it was. The hair thing again. I slithered across my hardwood floor to the window. Feeling like a CIA operative, a love spy, I threw myself against the wall, wedged between my dresser and the window. Cloaked by shadows, I pulled open the musky velvet curtain, the color of burgundy wine, and slowly cranked the closed window open so that I could witness what I hoped would be a full-fledged fight.

"I already told her we'd come." Antwone held his ground.

"Well, that's too bad, because I already made plans for us."

"Well, unmake them," Antwone said, annoyed. "Because I promised Camille I'd be there. Man's only as good as his word, baby girl."

Now if Gina had been there, the minute Antwone called M– "baby girl" she would have gotten on her high horse and said, "I told you so" big time. But the tenor of his voice gave me hope. Because when he called M– "baby girl," he sounded insincere. Antwone did not like confrontation; he saved all his fight for the football field, so I was not surprised that he tried to smooth things over with his difficult girlfriend by throwing a casual term of endearment her impossible way.

I snuck a glance out of the window just in time to see M– purposefully turn, posing herself in the pale moonlight. She draped her body against the column at the north end of the stoop to show her curvy figure to its full advantage.

The girl knew what she was doing, and the effect of her beauty was not lost on Antwone. I could sense him wavering, drinking in her sex like it was a Pat O'Brien hurricane. And

I didn't blame him; I understood his attraction to her. Even Beano thought she was hot. I had never been into girl-on-girl action, even though Gina and I once staged an impressive piece of lipstick love, a pretend kiss that Beano posted on Facebook. Kissing my best friend was a bold move, and although I recognized its cultural cache, posting the photo made me uncomfortable; it felt a little like false advertising. And when a sophomore on the water polo team made a pass at me, I deleted it. Still, if ever I were to try a for-real kiss with a girl, I could see myself experimenting with M—, which gives you some idea of the hypnotic effect she had on both men and women if even I, who detested her thoroughly, could fantasize about kissing her.

No, I did not blame Antwone for wanting to sleep with her; the problem was that like most guys his age, he confused desire with love.

"Can we save this fight for morning?" Antwone asked, leaning in to nibble her neck.

"We cannot," M— said, pulling away.

Antwone's sigh of resignation was audible. I guess he knew better than to push sex until he settled the issue of me. And I won't pretend that it didn't feel damn good to be an issue, a thorn in their rosy relationship.

"What you got against Camille anyway?"

"Don't act like you don't know," M— said.

"You're the one who's acting and what you're acting is crazy."

"I got eyes. That's all I'm saying."

"Yes, you do. And they are fine, fine, fine."

"Don't use that tone of voice with me."

"Girl, what are you talking about?"

"I'm talking about the way you drop down an octave to that soft, sexy place when you dish out compliments."

"I don't understand, baby. I thought you liked it when I talk like that."

"No, I *love* it when you talk like that to me. But when I

overheard you on the stoop, talking that way to Camille, I wanted to kick your ass all the way uptown."

"Ah hell, M–, I was just making conversation."

"You were flirting with her," M– said, all huffy-like.

I had been right; he was flirting with me. And the best part was that when M– accused him, he didn't deny it. He didn't make excuses or any of that. My heart was beating so fast I thought it might fly out of my chest and soar high atop the granite and glass of Place St. Charles on Canal.

And then he said, "Sweetie girl, why you so upset? You know I don't do white girls. I like a little coffee in my cream."

In all the years we had known each other, how had I missed that important piece of information? The night was turning into a cautionary tale about what could happen when you listened in on other people's lives. I knew I should leave—get out of there quick—but my feet refused to move, like they were glued to the hardwood floor. And when your feet won't go, you are, for all practical purposes, stuck. And so I stayed, even though it hurt to hear what came next.

"And it's not just Camille. You talk like that to all the girls."

"You must stay up all night, making this stuff up," Antwone said.

"Oh yeah? Well, what about Sondra Kincaid?" M– asked.

"What about her?"

"I saw you at her locker last week, buzzing all over her, talking trash."

"I needed help with calculus. Go ahead—accuse me of cheating on my homework, but I have never cheated on you."

"I want to believe you, but I can't," M– continued, detailing his every transgression girl-by-girl. As I listened, I felt oddly torn between my assumptions and her presumptions. The Antwone I knew was not a player. Still, I had to admit that she was certainly right about his affection for me. And technically speaking, every single time Antwone called *me* "baby girl," he was cheating on her. But as for the others, I couldn't get my head wrapped around that. And the more I thought about it, the more certain I became that she was dead wrong about there being other girls; it was against his nature. I was the only one he loved, even if the color of my skin was getting in the way of his knowing it yet.

"Look, baby, I'm not a player," Antwone said. "Sure, there are those girls who are willing to do things to me, with me, for me—you know what I'm talking about. But Camille is not one of them, and I don't mess around with the others. Not Jana who left her skanky black thong in my locker. Or the sophomore who sexted me a photo of her tits. Or Andrea who said she'd do me after I scored two touchdowns against Loyola and, for the record, I made three."

"You are the worst kind of player imaginable," M— replied. "You think that just because you keep your pants on, that makes you faithful. But you cheat on me every time you open your mouth."

"That is just bullshit. There is no one else, M—." Antwone pulled her to him.

"Be careful. Because I can smell the lie all over you," she said, sitting down on the porch swing beside him, leaning in, her nose close to his freshly laundered white tee.

"I love you, M—, but I'm tired of explaining myself to you. You've got to start trusting me or else—"

"Or what?"

"Or else there's no point to us."

I flung aside the heavy curtain to get a better look. I had to remind myself to breathe.

"You know, Antwone," M— began, brushing his cheek with the tips of her slender fingers. She threw her head back with a sigh and looked past him to my house.

And that's when she saw me, face pressed to the window, staring back at her. You know the old saying, "for what seemed like an eternity"? Well, that was exactly how long she and I locked into each other's gaze.

"When you are right, you are not wrong," she said. "There is no point to us. No point at all."

Then she kissed him goodbye.

༄

"I have never seen anybody so happy about somebody else being so miserable," Beano said as he shepherded me through the towering aisles of paper goods at Party City Thursday afternoon. "God is going to punish you."

As we sorted through a rainbow selection of colored paper plates, Beano told me that Antwone had had the worst practice of his illustrious career the morning after the break-up with M–. Ignoring him, I picked up a package of deep purple eleven-inch dinner plates, imagining how dramatic they would look on white tablecloths. Being a Mardi Gras baby, I am deeply fond of purple. It's a mysterious, spiritual color, made by combining opposites, hot red with cool blue. They say if you surround yourself with purple, you will have peace of mind. I threw four packages into the shopping cart and moved on to cups.

We argued over the virtue of paper versus plastic (Beano won) and as I tossed plastic tumblers into the shopping cart, Beano tried to convince me that Antwone was still in love with M–. "Do not think for one minute that just because M– is temporarily out of the picture, you can slip right into that girlfriend position. Because no way is St. Bede's most perfect couple gonna stay broken up. I'm not saying that before they get back together, he won't try to score a little something-something on the rebound, but you don't want to be that girl."

"I'm tired of people telling me what kind of girl I want to be. Especially you. This conversation is officially over."

We shopped in silence and, two hundred dollars poorer, we left the air-conditioned party bliss behind, stepped through the store's automated doors, and braced ourselves. It was so hot that the tar on the asphalt parking lot rose up in liquid bubbles that popped under our sandals. We zipped across the strip mall parking lot and quickly loaded up Beano's Hyundai with our party loot.

Gina met us in her front yard and helped us unload the sacks from the trunk. As we carried the last of them into the kitchen, her mom, whom we all called *The* Betsy, swooped in from the front part of the house, dressed up in a St. John knit sweater suit and pearls, which she considered everyday clothes.

The Betsy and I were uniquely connected; both of us shared our name with a famous hurricane. I was named after Hurricane Camille, a cat-five storm, the worst of the 1969 season, years before I was born. But according to Gina, Hurricane Betsy, one of the costliest hurricanes to hit the States, was actually named *after* her mother. Beano was first to add "The" to Betsy, because he said she deserved a title and Queen Mother was already taken.

I have been fascinated by Gina's mom ever since I witnessed her tell a salesclerk at Neiman Marcus that she adored the skirt of a two-thousand-dollar outfit but that the jacket terrified her. As far as I was concerned, any woman who would admit to being terrified of one-half of a two-piece suit was worthy of attention.

"Well, let's see what you kids bought," she said.

We lined up ready for inspection. The Betsy peeked into the first bag and practically shrieked.

"Did you buy the Orlando Bloom piñata when I wasn't looking?" I accused Beano, who shook his head vehemently.

As The Betsy grabbed the end of the butcher-block island to steady herself, Gina rifled through the bag and pulled out the offending merchandise. "Plastic cups? Seriously?" She held them up as if they were evidence in a murder trial.

"Shit, Beano, I told you we should have gone with paper," I said, using the one expletive allowed in the mansion on St. Charles. According to The Betsy, "shit" was the only acceptable cussword a lady would use. All others were strictly prohibited.

"Fuck," Gina said, who only used the f-word in front of

her mother just to annoy her. "Paper would have been worse. Mother only recently broke her moratorium against *paper* napkins."

Still reeling, The Betsy straightened herself and walked over to the small writing desk in the corner of the kitchen, where many an elaborate party plan had been hatched. She gingerly opened a cloisonné box and pulled out a Virginia Slim, which she lit with a fourteen-carat gold lighter that once belonged to a New Orleans madam who killed herself in the streets of the Quarter. More than once, Gina had pointed out the implicit irony in her mother committing symbolic suicide by lighting her "cancer stick" with a lighter that had belonged to someone who had quite deliberately done herself in. But The Betsy blew away her daughter's protests with the same casual style she used to exhale the smoke, claiming she only smoked to calm her nerves, as if that erased any possible health risk. As she sucked the smoke up her nose in a steady stream, she turned her attention back to the issue of the cups.

"Camille, honey, I'm not about to pull out my Saint Louis goblets for a kid's birthday party but plastic cups are just plain unacceptable. There are many reasons God made cheap crystal and your birthday is just one of them. We have never used plastic cups in this house, not even in a hurricane."

The Betsy was a master at transforming bad weather into a social opportunity. When a tropical storm threatened, a few folks would leave town, but The Betsy always stayed put, boarding up her windows and opening up her doors to like-minded neighbors to ride out the storm. Her motto was: "When it's raining cats and dogs, you can't get any work done. You might as well make a little cocktail, open up a jar of caviar, and have a little visit."

And evidently, she used the good glasses.

The Betsy stubbed out her cigarette and unpacked glass punch cups that Beano and I dutifully washed even though they were put away perfectly clean. And while we dried the cups by hand, Betsy entertained us with stories of perfect parties and ones that fell short.

"My favorite was a Twelfth Night at the St. Louis Hotel Vieux Carre on Bienville Street. I was nineteen at the time. It was given for my cousin Margaret, my mother's sister's daughter who was born on Epiphany."

Given my own auspicious beginnings and that particular Twelfth Night story, I perked up, interested to hear hers.

"Margaret was absolutely gorgeous. Ethereal-looking. Her skin was so porcelain white, it was practically translucent. And her daddy, my Uncle Bill, a Williams and from the moneyed branch of the family tree, absolutely adored her. So when she turned twenty-one, well, you can just imagine. Her mother had the hotel's lush courtyard draped with a canopy of gardenias. The smell was positively intoxicating. Everybody was there, daughters and sons from all the good families—feasting on shrimp, crab, and platters of oysters on the half shell and guzzling Dom Perignon like it was keg beer. There wasn't a single crumb left from the King Cake's, which came from McKenzies, of course. I cried buckets when they went out of business. Everybody said they made the best dough in Louisiana and nobody was lying. But I digress."

She paused, reflecting on something far more personal and private than the memory of the sugary treasure from McKenzies. I worried she might have changed her mind about telling us what was sure to be the best part of the story. Finally, she spoke.

"That night I made the most eligible bachelor in the whole of Orleans Parish—your father—fall in love with me. I'd been trying for months to get his attention and I had not succeeded. He only had eyes for Margaret, which was maddening because I knew she didn't love him; she was in love with his pedigree. That was the only reason she agreed to marry him. I could see that it would never work out between the two of them. Because I had mined the depths of his soul and knew he and I were meant for each other and, if given half a chance, we would have a wonderful marriage. Which we did," she said, lighting another Virginia Slim, "until we didn't."

"I cannot believe I did not know this. Daddy was engaged to Cousin Maggie?"

"Well, yes. I mean, she had a ring. But it wasn't as if they had sent out engraved invitations. They hadn't even set a date for the wedding."

"I don't believe you. How could you flat-out steal your cousin's fiancé?" Gina asked, upset.

"Well, it wasn't easy," The Betsy said, misconstruing her daughter's concern. "I had to enlist help."

"From who?" I asked.

"I can't tell you that," The Betsy said, taking a long drag from her cigarette.

"Well, you might as well, since you've gone this far. Jeez, I feel like I was adopted or something," Gina said, trying to make sense of this new genealogical intel.

"I can't tell you because I swore not to. Strong magic has its cost. Never forget that."

"Are you saying you used magic to make him fall in love with you?" Beano asked.

"I'm saying magic opened his eyes to the possibility of loving me. It was up to me to do the heavy lifting," The Betsy said, correcting him.

"What kind of magic? You have to tell us. Seriously, I have to know. Did you use a love potion?" I asked, breathlessly.

"Heavens no. Love potions are for amateurs. The kind of voodoo magic I'm talking about you can't buy online."

"If not online, then where?"

The Betsy stopped, stubbed out her cigarette, realizing that she had revealed more than she intended. "That's all I'm gonna say."

"One more question. Please," I begged.

I felt the disapproving stares of my two best friends. They knew why I was asking.

"Where can you find"—I used air quotes for emphasis—"the kind of voodoo magic you're talking about?"

"Well, you have to go directly to the source. A voodoo queen. Problem is the powerful ones are all dead."

❧

"I think I may have wasted fifteen dollars and ninety-nine cents," I told Beano as we left the house, revealing my visit to, and purchase from, Miss Fleurette.

He stared at me for a long time, as if he were measuring the depth of my commitment. Satisfied that he could not talk me out of love, he let out a dramatic sigh.

"Forget about voodoo. You got me, and I know a thing or two about getting a man. Come on, *baby girl*, we're going shopping."

"For what?"

"Sexy underwear."

To tell the truth, up until that point, I hadn't given my panties a second thought.

He continued, "What you put next to skin is crucial. You gotta choose something that not only looks hot but makes you feel sexy. It's seduction from the inside out."

"Give me a little credit. You act like I was planning on wearing Batman boxer shorts."

Beano gave me that look. "Well, Camille, you do own a pair."

Once Beano decided he could not talk me out of love, he committed himself wholeheartedly to transforming me into the kind of woman Antwone would not be able to resist. But instead of taking me to Victoria's Secret in the mall, Beano drove me uptown to Miss Bea's Boutique. In the window were two towering mannequins, the first in a see-through bra, the other in a leather bustier and whip. The entire window was framed with crotchless panties hanging from a clothesline.

I balked. But Beano pushed me inside before I could protest. A male salesclerk who bore an uncanny resemblance to Lady Gaga approached. "Can I help you?"

Right in front of me was a rack of thick-looking panties,

which seemed out of place in this sexed-up place. "What are those?" I asked.

"Nothing you need, sweetie," he replied. "They're called gaffs, and they're designed to hide the boy parts."

"They look uncomfortable," Beano observed.

"Oh, honey, you have no idea," he said. "They can be killer if you're in an arousing situation, if you know what I mean. Like I always say, it's best to avoid hot men when you're tucked."

Words to live by.

He directed me to the backroom, which stocked ladies' sizes. Beano found a pair of black lacy thongs, which I rejected, based on Jana's having left a pair in Antwone's locker. I also said no to a red velvet thong with a teensy, weensy glittery crotch, because it looked itchy.

Frustrated, Beano got a little testy. He clearly disapproved of me disapproving. "This is beyond fabulous," he said, holding up a persimmon-colored push-up bra with scattered rhinestones on the skinny double straps and a matching thong. "Guaranteed to channel your inner goddess."

I decided to trust him. After all, Beano, like the city we grew up in, knew the secret of turning pleasure into fine art.

By the time I got home, it was early evening, around six, which according to my daddy, is the saddest hour of the day. He says people get depressed when the sun sets because they are thrown into a kind of purgatory: the transition between the death of a day and the birth of a night. He's fond of pointing out that the cocktail hour was invented to ease that transition, to help people let go of the day's worries so they could embrace the dark.

As I walked up my steps, I saw Antwone sitting on the porch swing, the very one where he and M— had broken up the night before. He reminded me of those old men you see when you drive out toward Breaux Bridge into the swamplands—the ones who sit and swing like they got nothing better to do than watch the rest of the world zoom by.

"Want some company?" I asked.

He nodded and I crossed the yard to join him. Sharing an old porch swing with another person requires the two of you to work in tandem, kicking off with your feet at the same time, allowing gravity to take you backward and push you forward. It is a surprisingly intimate experience. Antwone's arm rested on the back of the swing, his hand only inches away from my shoulder. I was intensely aware that our thighs were near touching. As we rocked back and forth, lulled by the creaking iron chain and the chirping cicadas, a Category 1 hurricane made its first landfall in Florida near Hallandale Beach on the Dade County line. She was named Katrina.

4.

I always thought you were a nice girl," my mother said accusingly, holding up the bra and thong from Miss Bea's. Evidently, the smell of lavender from the scented signature bag aroused her suspicion. And on the Friday evening before my birthday party, she followed her nose and found the contraband hidden under my bed.

"You have no right to go through my stuff," I answered, praying she had not found the bottle of love potion as well.

"I do, as long as you live in my house. And I will not have a daughter of mine wearing trashy underwear."

Just then my cell rang and I stepped out of the argument and into the hallway. Gina told me that the storm was expected to make landfall on Sunday morning and that the governor had just declared a state of emergency. Neither of my own parents had mentioned it, so I didn't think it was a big deal. During hurricane season, states of emergencies were as common as dirt. But Gina went on to explain that while her mother had decided to stay in New Orleans and ride out the storm NO MATTER WHAT, my Saturday night birthday party was eighty-sixed.

I hung up and immediately called Beano so we could come up with Party Plan B. But he was in the middle of boxing up his collection of Broadway musical vinyls. He lived with his grandmother, who was visiting a friend in New York, so his dad stepped up in a rare act of parental responsibility to spirit Beano away with his stepmom and his three-year-old half-brother Kemper to a cousin's house in New Iberia. I should have known that they would be the first to leave. Beano's stepmom was from Boston and the mere whisper of a hurricane terrified her.

I gave up. My birthday had effectively been cancelled.

I marched back into the bedroom where my mother waited. I yanked the bra away from her, grabbed the thong off the bed, and threw the whole kit and caboodle into the trash.

"There," I screamed at my mother, "are you satisfied now?"

She sighed. "Well, that's just being wasteful, Camille."

Sometimes there is no satisfying my mother.

As soon as she left, I unearthed the love potion from my underwear drawer, retreated into the bathroom, and poured the contents into the toilet bowl. I pulled the chain and literally flushed my elaborate scheme to win Antwone's heart down the toilet.

I slept fitfully that night and awoke Saturday to a flurry of activity; my parents—who apparently knew all about the storm but decided not to worry me—were getting the house ready for it. Around ten, I left with my father for the French Quarter to board up the plate glass windows in the bar. He told my mother to fill up the car while we were gone. Just in case we had to get out quick.

"Turn up the radio, Camille," my daddy hollered as he nailed the plywood to the shutters and strapped down additional clips from the roof to the frame of the building to prevent roof damage. While we worked, the warnings kept building; residents of low-lying communities such as Algiers and the Ninth Ward were told to leave immediately.

Later at dinner, I asked what we were going to do. Leave or stay?

Mary Ellen put down her fork and tensed up like a skittish cat. Since the day she first met my father in Jackson Square, she would only leave the parish of New Orleans for weddings and funerals. She belonged to that class of people who came to New Orleans for a vacation and never left. When her own mother criticized her for giving up that promising job in Houston to marry my father and help run a bar, she said, "I didn't give up my career. I chose my life."

Daddy took a last bite of chicken-fried steak, sopped up the gravy with the corner of his biscuit, and changed the subject. "So how long did you have to wait at the gas station? Were the lines very long?" he asked.

"I'm sorry. I got preoccupied and forgot to gas up the car."

"Are you kidding me? You did not forget," I said.

"Camille!" they both yelled in unison. I couldn't believe how they both turned on me when she was the one who had screwed up.

My father grabbed his keys, saying he would take care of it himself. He left, and my mother declared war on the dirty dishes. She scraped the plates so hard, I thought they might break. After cleaning up the kitchen, she poured herself a stiff drink and went across the street to see our neighbor, Adele, a fifth-generation New Orleanian. Her house was about four times as big as ours. Her dining room was lined with thirty feet of cabinets full of sterling silver serving dishes, all of it from family. My mother always brought her own cocktail to her friend's house because she didn't want to appear like she was asking for a free ride from the richest lady in the neighborhood.

Daddy returned a full hour and a half later, dog-tired. When my mother reported that the folks across the street had decided to stay, he just said, "I don't want to fight about this tonight."

So my parents left the question of whether to leave or whether to stay hanging in the hot, muggy air and went to bed with the firm resolve to discuss it in the morning.

Early the next day, on Sunday, I wandered into the kitchen where Mary Ellen was scrambling up some eggs. I started to turn on the television, but she stopped me. "You know we don't allow TV at the meal table unless it's a Saints football game."

"Or a hurricane in the making," my Daddy said, correcting her. "Turn it on, Camille."

On screen, our smooth-talking mayor said we were "facing the storm most of us have feared." With winds howling across the Gulf at 145 miles per hour, he issued a mandatory evacuation for the entire parish of New Orleans.

"Well, that settles that," my father said. "Mary Ellen, you and Camille pack up. Last night I called Cousin Henri in St. Martinville and he said the two of you could stay with them until the storm blows over."

Mary Ellen slapped runny eggs on his plate. "What about you?"

Daddy straightened himself into an official-looking pose, like he was the president or something. "You know what comes after a storm. Somebody's got to stay at the bar to protect it from looters."

"I can wave a pistol in the air just as good as you," Mary Ellen insisted. "People are lots more scared of me than they are of you."

"You mean people we know."

"I mean people. Period. Honey, I love you, but you are not very intimidating."

I had to admit, she had a point.

Mary Ellen continued, "Either we all go to Cajun country or we all go down to the bar. But I'm not leaving without you."

"Do you really want to put your daughter in harm's way when the looting starts?"

If he thought he could manipulate Mary Ellen into evacuating New Orleans by appealing to her maternal instincts, he was dead wrong. They fought like never before; their voices rose like a hurricane wind threatening to blow the roof off their marriage. But right when my mother was about to say something that she could never take back, a loud knock at the front of the house interrupted her.

My daddy threw open the door, surprised to find Antwone, who looked just about as frustrated as my father felt. Behind him stood Bama, clutching her pearl-handled overnight suitcase.

"You hear about the evacuation?" he asked.

"We sure did," Daddy answered. "Camille and her mom were just about to pack up a few things and get on the road. They're gonna stay with my cousins in St. Martinville."

"Can you take Bama with you?" Antwone asked.

He explained that the night before, he'd called Bama's ninety-year-old sister, Auntie Shay, in the Ninth Ward and told her they'd be by in the morning to pick her up. But by daybreak, Auntie Shay, who collected feral cats, had changed her mind; she couldn't leave town because her favorite kitty, a small tabby named King Oliver, was missing.

Antwone ushered Bama into the living room with my mother so he could have a more private word with my father.

"I can deal with one old lady and nine cats, but two old ladies are just one too many. I'm thinking if your wife could take Bama, I'll go down to the Ninth Ward, take care of this cat-astrophe and catch up with them in St. Martinville. From there, I can drive the old ladies on over to my great-auntie's place in Lafayette."

Back in the living room, Mary Ellen knew Fate had made the decision for us. We were leaving. My mother might throw me under the bus, but she'd never put Bama, whom she adored more than her own mother, in harm's way. She slipped out of the room to throw a few things in a suitcase, and I stepped out on the porch to say goodbye to Antwone.

"Do you want me to go with you? I could help with the cats and I'm sure Mary Ellen wouldn't mind."

"And I'm sure your daddy would."

When animals sensed the coming of a storm, they often disappeared, sometimes for days. What if Antwone wasn't able to find Auntie Shay's beloved King Oliver? Then what?

"Auntie Shay is almost as stubborn as your own momma," he said, leaning closer to me, "but I can be very convincing."

"Promise me if King Oliver isn't on the stoop by the time you get there, you'll throw that old woman over your shoulder and carry her out."

Antwone laughed, trying to picture it. Auntie Shay was as fat as Bama was thin. She weighed over two hundred and fifty pounds and was not easy to transport.

"Okay, I promise if you promise me something."

"I'd do anything for you, Antwone. You know that."

"Thing is, even though we're broke up, I worry about M—. And with all this hurricane business—" he stopped, as if figuring it out for himself. "If this storm's as bad as they say, and if for some reason I'm unable to, will you look out for her?"

What was I thinking? Making a promise without knowing the terms. Now I was as morally stuck as my feet had been the night I listened in on their break-up.

"M—'s a lot stronger than you think she is," I said.

"No, she's not. She acts tough, but she's as delicate as a butterfly's wing."

"Well, maybe I'm not as strong as you think I am."

"Yeah, you are," Antwone said, stepping to the side as a five-inch roach scampered across the porch and into the ferns. "Just like that palmetto bug."

I did not like the way this insect metaphor was heading. Palmetto bug was a fancy name for TREE ROACH, the vilest, ugliest, most disgusting creature on earth. As far as I knew they serve not one useful purpose. The night they broke up, M— said Antwone had stung her with his words. So he was a bee, M— was a butterfly, and I was a damn tree roach.

Antwone could see I was upset, so he tried to smooth over the comparison.

"You ever try to kill a palmetto bug? It's impossible 'cause they're engineered to survive," he said. "That's why they remind me of you."

And then it happened—the thing I had mentally rehearsed about a hundred times before. But when it finally came to pass, I didn't think at all. I acted and the act of it was as natural as breathing. I reached up and kissed him. Or he kissed me. I wasn't quite sure who started it or who pulled away first. All I knew for certain was that his lips tasted sweet, a trace of syrup from the French toast he had for breakfast.

He took me in his arms and held me tight, the smell of him seeping into my skin. We held each other for a long time and when he pulled away, I shuddered, overcome by another feeling—passion replaced by dread and forewarning, like a cosmic clue from the universe. I was suddenly aware that the people I loved most would soon be separated from me, facing the storm of the century on their own. And people would die. I had a horrible feeling that somebody I loved would be among them. I grabbed Antwone's arm as he started to leave.

"I don't want you to go without me," I said.

"The sooner I leave, the sooner I can get on the road."

"I'm scared."

"Don't be. Everything's gonna turn out fine."

"Promise?"

"I swear it."

Relieved, I shook off my premonition. In all of the years that I had known Antwone, he'd never made a promise he couldn't keep.

5.

By the time we left town, it was way too late to get out quick. The wind had picked up and a light rain began to fall. Traffic wasn't too bad on surface roads, but when Mary Ellen pulled off Basin Street and merged onto the I-10, we slowed to a crawl. We joined a river of headlights streaming toward higher ground, leaving the city that care forgot. I was wedged in the back seat between what we had to take and what we couldn't live without. On my left were two gallons of water, an old metal suitcase of family mementoes, a bag of sweet potato fries, and Bama's cooler full of crawfish. Don't ask me why, but nobody evacuates New Orleans in a hurricane without a goodly supply of seafood.

On my right was an elaborate beaded, feathered suit hand-sewn by Bama's late husband, Big Chief Tito of the Wild Tchoupitoulas. In the early days, when Black neighborhoods formed their own Mardi Gras krewes, because the white folks wouldn't let them into theirs, they named themselves after Indian tribes to honor their Native American brothers and sisters who had given sanctuary to runaway slaves. Back then, there was fierce competition between the tribes on Fat Tuesday that often turned ugly. Mardi Gras became a day to settle scores in the street.

Now it was more like a sewing contest. The costume sitting next to me was massive; it weighed over two hundred pounds. When I was nine, Bama took Antwone and me to see Big Chief Tito dance through the Treme. I remember his coming up against a Big Chief from another tribe, the two of them showing off their beadwork like two roosters sizing each other up before a cock fight. It was something to see. That night, Tito asked Antwone if he wanted to be a Big Chief one day. He said no, that he'd rather be a Spy Boy. "I want to be the one in front of the tribe, looking out for trouble. Spy Boys are the baddest of all the Indians."

Tito told him that only a chosen few got to be Spy Boys, that it was a big responsibility to send out a signal when another tribe was approaching and to announce the arrival of his own Big Chief. Antwone couldn't wait to take on the mantle. But that never happened. Life got in the way. Tito had a heart attack and died before the next Mardi Gras.

As Mary Ellen drove, her hands clenched on the steering wheel, Bama and I made small talk about little things like St. Bede's chances for a city football championship. Bama might have been hard-of-hearing, but she was easy to talk to, and while I can't say that time flew, it did pass amicably. As we crossed I-55 and put Lake Pontchartrain in our rearview mirror, a breaking news bulletin came on the radio. A blustery bigwig from Jefferson Parish announced: "Mark my word, we are in the beginnings of the storm forecasters have predicted for years—the nightmare scenario for New Orleans. Those who have decided to stay and ride out the storm are just plain fools—diehards who will DIE HARD."

Mary Ellen slammed her fist on the dashboard and the radio miraculously turned off. I was pretty much convinced that her resolve to "stay positive, no matter what" had effectively silenced the airwaves.

But from that point on, nobody really had anything much to say. About three hours into our ride, which should have taken two and half hours tops and took a full eight, I got a text from Antwone, which I read out loud. He was making one more round in the neighborhood to look for King Oliver and after that they would be on their way out. He ended with: *Don't wait dinner but save a little something for me and Auntie Shay.*

Bama laughed out loud. "It'll take more than a little

something-something to satisfy those two. Auntie Shay is what my momma called 'a good eater.'"

I texted him back that I'd save more for him than a big plate of crawfish étouffée. And then I drifted off to sleep in the back seat of our SUV with Tito's feathered headdress as my pillow.

When I woke, it was dark. As we turned a corner, I could see the street sign in our headlights and, for a moment, I imagined myself back home on Poydras Street near the St. James Hotel. But then I realized I wasn't on *that* Poydras Street. I was deep in Cajun country, in St. Martinville, which lies on the Bayou Teche, a little town of seven thousand with strong French roots. My daddy's first cousin, Henri, said that we Darveaus were not Cajuns but pure-blooded Acadians, because we could trace our lineage back to the first exiled families from French-speaking Canada. Henri criticized my daddy mightily because I could only speak rudimentary French. Henri's three daughters, ages fourteen, twelve, and six, grew up speaking what they considered "their native tongue." Henri bragged that his girls didn't even learn English until they went to kindergarten, as if that were a good thing.

Henri spent his whole life on a factory line making peppers into hot sauce for the Bulliard family. In order to understand how a man like that could become such a cultural snob, you'd have to spend a helluva lot of time in the bayou.

We pulled into Henri's driveway at eight. St. Martinville had many grand buildings with beautiful architecture, but Henri's home was not one of them. His was mobile-manufactured, which meant the house had been prefabricated in a factory and hauled on a trailer to the building site. Henri loved to point out that it looked just like a proper built-from-the-ground-up home at half the cost. But I disagreed. If Henri was a genealogy snob, I was an architectural one. Like my daddy, I preferred buildings with real foundations, and I knew that underneath the crisp white siding of Henri's mobile-manufactured home was a dou-blewide that belonged in a trailer park.

"Hiya doin', cher?" Henri's wife, Jeannette, shouted as we emptied out of the car and onto the front lawn.

I loved Jeannette. She was as open-hearted as Henri was close-minded. She gave me a big hug, then turned to Bama and welcomed her like she was New Orleans royalty. Even my mother's Texas roots were forgiven in her warm hello. Although we hadn't seen them for several years, we were embraced like we were the closest of families and ushered into the house where my cousins were setting the table for a fantastic spread. Jeannette believed that food was not a poor substitute for love; it was love itself. We set down at the table to a basket of Louisiana blue crabs, their spiny shells turned bright orange-red, a platter of rosy crawfish tails cooked in their own juices with onions, cayenne, corn, and potatoes, and bowls of rich brown gumbo teeming with seasoned sausage.

"Eat, eat, *a bon cour*," Jeannette urged. "Then tonight, we make the *veiller*," which roughly translated to "Eat up and then we'll visit." Jeannette spoke with a decided Acadian patois, a linguistic gumbo of its own.

Although I was not hungry, I ate plenty, knowing that no matter how much we consumed, there would be plenty left for Antwone and Auntie Shay.

After dinner, Henri flipped on CNN just as a reporter announced he was reporting live from the French Quarter.

"Quarter, my ass. He's standing on Magazine," my mother exclaimed, blowing up for about the fourth time that day, if anybody was counting. Not to offend my younger cousins, she quickly added, "Excuse my French."

The girls pulled back, appalled. Saying "ass" was perfectly fine, but a true Darveau would never use the word "French" as a metaphor for cursing.

"Why is Aunt Mary Ellen so upset?" six-year-old Feola asked.

"Anybody who knows anything about New Orleans knows

that in the Quarter, Magazine Street is called Decatur," I explained.

"And St. Charles is Royal," my mother added.

"And Camp becomes Chatres. I could go on and on but that would just be showing off."

Feola screwed up her face, puzzled, and asked, "Why do the same streets have different names? It's confusing."

"Not if you live there," I said. "And the why is what makes it interesting. You see, the Creoles were so pissed when the Americans began pouring in after the Purchase, they built Canal Street, which was supposed to be an actual canal with water. But that didn't work out so they had to settle for a big wide boulevard instead. On the lakeside of Canal is the French Quarter; on the riverside is the American sector. And the Creoles wouldn't even let the Americans use the same street names."

"And that man," yelled my mother, pointing at the newscaster like he was the Wicked Witch of the West, "is *not* standing in the Quarter."

About an hour later and after my mother finally calmed down, good news came at last. They said that Katrina might pass to the east of New Orleans. We cheered like we were at a Saints game. Maybe we had been saved.

At ten, my daddy called; he'd been trying to get through for hours. At our urging, Mary Ellen put him on speakerphone, and as we circled round, Bama said it reminded her of how people in the forties gathered around the radio to listen to President Roosevelt's fireside chats.

Donald laughed and said he would try hard to be as reassuring as the late president.

"I don't want to be reassured," Mary Ellen said. "If I should be worried, I want to know."

"No need for any of that," Donald said, and he told us that it had started to rain hard, but he was tucked away safe in the bar with half a dozen of his best customers—diehards who, like him, had refused to evacuate.

Mary Ellen's eyes flashed with emotion at the very mention. I squeezed her hand to calm her down.

Donald went on to explain that he had enlisted the skills of my cross-dressing math tutor, Anita Cocktail.

"So what is Miz Cocktail gonna do? Put on a floor show for your little hurricane party?" my mother asked.

"What's a floor show?" Feola asked.

"Miz Cocktail's a drag queen who performs twice a week at the Bourbon Pub and Parade. She's very talented," I explained.

"What's a Bourbon Pub and Parade?" asked Delphine, my middle cousin who had long straight hair the color of polished copper.

"A gay bar featuring Southern Decadence," I answered, quoting the signage on the front of the bar.

"What's Southern Decadence?" asked Feola.

"It's a special chocolate dessert with whipped cream and nuts. I believe I even have the recipe," Jeannette said, hoping to put that conversation to rest.

Meanwhile, Donald tried to put something else to rest—Mary Ellen's reservations.

"We're not putting on a floor show, and we're not having a party. But I did ask Miss Cocktail to count out shots and keep track of bottles, so things don't get out of hand."

"I don't care what you say. It sounds like a party to me," Mary Ellen said. "Wish I was there."

"I do too, honey, but you did what you had to do and I'm proud of you. Has Antwone gotten there yet with Auntie Shay?"

"No, but he was at least three hours behind us," I said.

"Getting out of town was a mess. It could take them twice as long as us," my mother said.

"I wouldn't worry," Donald said. "Cell towers are overpowered. Took me forever to get through to you."

The last thing my daddy said to Henri before signing off was, "Thanks for taking care of my three gorgeous girls. See to it that they stay out of trouble."

Bama was pleased to be called a "girl" at her age and tickled that he thought her young enough to get into trouble.

"Your husband is a flirt," she told Mary Ellen.

"So is your grandson," Mary Ellen teased. And they wrapped their arms around each other. We all allowed ourselves to believe that everything would be okay, when in fact, nothing would ever be the same again.

After we hung up, Jeannette stood to usher her daughters and me off to bed. "Time to *fais do, mi petite gaiennes.*"

I protested; it was only eleven and I wanted to stay up until Antwone and Auntie Shay got there. Mary Ellen, who was bunking on a couch in the living room, promised to wake me the minute they arrived. Marguerite, who was Jeanette's oldest and just a couple of years younger than me, gave up her bedroom to Bama, who swore that she didn't mind sleeping on a couch or a chair.

"One of the benefits of getting old is you can sleep anywhere. Your bones don't mind. They gonna ache when you get up no matter where you lie down."

"No, MawMaw, you get the bed," Jeannette insisted. I watched as she settled Bama into her eldest daughter's room, changing the sheets, picking up the clutter, and placing a glass of water in her best crystal on the bedside table in case Bama woke up thirsty. I was so grateful that Henri had married such a woman, whose kindness would make our temporary exile bearable.

But as Jeannette quietly closed the door to Marguerite's room and turned the corner to her own, I overheard her grumble to her husband, "This is one big mess of trouble. I guess we can put the two old ladies together in Marguerite's room. But where is the *bon a rien* gonna sleep when he gets here?"

I didn't know what a *bon a rien* was, but the tone of her voice bothered me. She sounded pissed off. I always believed Jeannette to be a genuine person, but now I wondered if her Southern hospitality was all a front. I slipped down the hall to the smallest of the three bedrooms where my three cousins were sorting the sleeping arrangements. Troubled, I asked Marguerite what a "*bon a rien*" was?

"A good-for-nothing, lazy man," she explained with a casual toss of her perfectly curled hair.

I felt like I'd been punched in the stomach. Jeannette had never met Antwone; she didn't know a damn thing about him. And yet she called him lazy and no-count. There was only one explanation, one that cut me to the core. She judged him unfairly just because he was Black. I had to swallow two hard, cold facts and they did not go down well. My favorite of all my daddy's Cajun cousins was not only two-faced but also a racist.

Her daughters made no pretense of fake Southern hospitality; they were put out at being put out, hurricane or no hurricane. The bossy Marguerite commandeered the top bunk, assigned her two sisters to the bottom one, and gave me the trundle, which was a child's bed and so short that my legs hung off mid-calf. As I attempted to situate myself, Feola crept up behind me, sticking her perfectly upturned nose close to my head. "Poo-yee. Do you smell dat? Stinks like a monkey. Maybe you got one hiding in there."

Well, that sent all three girls into a fit of giggles. But I was not amused. I stood up and leveled them with the one Cajun phrase I knew by heart: "*Beck moi tchew.*"

Bite my ass.

"For heavens' sakes, Camille, could you at least try to be nice?" my mother asked, standing at the door with an armload of towels. She had an uncanny knack for showing up at exactly the wrong moment.

As soon as she left the room, I grabbed a towel and announced that I would take the first shower because I wanted to clean up for Antwone. Marguerite turned to me, her milky blue eyes wide with false innocence. "I swear, Camille, you act like he's your boyfriend or something," she said in a snarky tone of voice intended to put me on the defensive.

It worked.

"I'm not acting," I said.

"Antwone isn't your boyfriend. It's not possible," Feola protested.

"Why not?"

"Because he's colored."

Oh my, this was going to be a long, long night.

I attempted to educate my youngest cousin because, unlike her older sisters, she was impressionable and of a sweet nature.

"Antwone is African American. You can call him Black or even Creole, if you prefer. But colored is a word you use to describe the stained glass in church windows, not people."

Marguerite wrapped her arm around her younger sister and stroked her hair affectionately as she turned on me. "Personally, Camille, I am totally surprised that you are hooking up with a boy at all. Since all you ever do is talk about gay bars and drag queen tutors, we assumed that you were a *lesbienne*."

"I am done explaining myself to a bunch of bayou hicks."

I grabbed two towels and left the room in a flashy show of attitude. Mostly I was angry with myself. I had managed to keep my crush a secret from my two best friends for years, but in a matter of minutes, Marguerite had goaded me into sharing my personal life with family I no longer trusted.

I took a long shower. The nozzle spray hit my back in a steady stream; frustration and worry gave way to watery daydreams.

Antwone would be here soon. We would have two whole days together, maybe even more if the storm lasted long enough. I was probably the only person in southeast Louisiana praying to stretch out bad weather.

I soaped my head a second time. My cousins were right about one thing: my hair was a mess. Aisha had left town the week before to visit her sick sister in Florida and had not been able to work me in before she left. A wave of guilt passed over me, like the storm making landfall. I had been so obsessed with my personal dramas that I completely ignored the fact that Katrina had passed through Florida last Thursday, not too far from where Aisha was staying with her sister. People had died in Florida. I remembered hearing that on the news. How many? That I couldn't recall. Maybe eight. Was it nine? Did the horrible premonition I had about death that morning mark Aisha's passing?

"Get out of that shower RIGHT NOW," Mary Ellen demanded, banging on the bathroom door. "Bama wants to talk to you."

Her voice startled me. If Bama was the one who wanted to *talk* to me, why did Mary Ellen sound so pissed off?

I hastily threw on boxers and a T-shirt and wrapped my hair in a towel. Summoned into the living room, I found Mary Ellen sitting on the sofa beside Bama, whose face was etched in quiet dismay.

"What's going on between you and Antwone?" Bama asked.

"What do you mean?" I answered, having learned that the best defense against a possible interrogation is to answer a question with another question. If nothing else, it will buy you time.

"Well, there are some people who say that he's your boyfriend," Mary Ellen added.

"What people?" I asked.

"Well, is he?" Bama asked, her voice trembling with anger. ANGER. My whole life, Bama had never, ever once been mad at me.

The two of them being so obviously upset about Antwone being my boyfriend didn't make any sense. Granted, we were in the South and my mother was from Texas, but we had been in each other's homes and lives for all of mine. I suddenly realized that maybe that was the problem; we were too close, like extended family.

"Are you upset because if the two of us were together, and I'm not saying we are but if we were, it would be like incest or something?"

"Do not use that filthy word in this house," Jeanette said,

eavesdropping from the hall. Our Acadian cousins were very sensitive on the subject of incest; I could only imagine why. Jeanette excused herself, saying she hoped Mary Ellen could settle this thing before that boy gets here. "Because I'm not going to have any of that going on in my house."

After she left, I turned back to Bama and Mary Ellen. "Why is everybody so upset? What's the big deal?"

My mother, who usually has an answer for everything, was strangely silent.

"It's just not right," Bama said, finally.

"What's not right?" I asked.

"For a Black boy to be involved with a white girl. Or vice versa," Bama said. "Both you and Antwone were raised better than that."

I turned to my mother. "Is that the way you feel, too?"

She looked down at the floor. "I think we have trouble enough in this house without complicating things with teenage drama."

Let me stop right here and point out that both Bama and my mother were liberal Democrats. They were broad-minded, smart, articulate women of two different generations who shared a passion for what was right and fair; they had fought for civil rights. I could not fathom how loving Antwone crossed a line I never even knew existed. I wanted to rewind and erase the last five minutes of my life.

A sea of silence separated us. Finally, Mary Ellen spoke: "I would hope that you and Antwone would consider how your being together would upset Bama."

"My momma always said it was a bad idea for the races to mix," Bama added.

"Well, then most of New Orleans has been involved in that 'bad idea' since before the Louisiana Purchase," I said, unable to contain myself. "There isn't a second-generation New Orleans family who doesn't have a little white or Black blood in there somewhere. I mean, look at me. Where do you think I got my hair?"

That hit a chord, oddly not as much with Bama as with Mary Ellen, who bristled at my audacity.

"It's one thing for you to disrespect me, young lady, but I will not allow you to use that tone when you speak to Bama. Do we understand each other?"

I nodded.

"I don't mind the sass, but you still haven't answered me," Bama said. "You and Antwone got something goin' on?"

If I told the truth, then Antwone would walk through the front door to a room full of accusations, which could scare him off from ever becoming my real boyfriend. So I rewrote the story.

"We do not," I said.

"Then why did Marguerite say you do?" my mother asked.

"Because I told her that we did," I answered.

"Why on earth would you say a thing like that?" Mary Ellen asked.

"Because she was going on and on about my being a lesbian. So I said that Antwone was my boyfriend to shut her up."

"Well, now that is a relief," Bama said. "I'm sorry, Camille. I always knew you were a good girl."

Stiff and sore from the drive, Bama said goodnight and tottered off to bed. I turned on my heels to follow, but Mary Ellen stopped me.

She held out her arms and invited me in for a hug. I knew that was her way of saying she was sorry.

"Do you honestly believe interracial dating is wrong?" I asked.

"Of course not."

I couldn't fathom why Mary Ellen hadn't tried to set Bama straight on the subject. Bama might be old and set in her ways, but if anyone could chisel away at the misguided notions of Bama's own mother, it was mine.

Mary Ellen's conciliatory gesture—her outstretched arms—only made her silence on the subject worse, so instead of accepting it, I walked past her down the hall and climbed into the child's bed that waited for me.

That night the whole house slept, fitfully for some, peacefully for others. I was too exhausted to stay up worrying or being mad. I passed out hard, dreaming of the one they said I shouldn't love.

6.

I woke the next morning to the peaceful swoosh of billowy curtains blowing in the light breeze. The yellow walls of my youngest cousin's bedroom were streaked with hazy sunlight, making the cheap prints of French landscapes look like real masterpieces. My legs ached from hanging off the bed. How long had I slept? I had no idea. Last night's drama had exhausted me. I was so dead to the world I didn't even turn over when my fussy cousins left for school. I dragged myself out of bed and into the den, where my mother, Bama, and Jeanette were glued to the TV.

"Where's Antwone?" I asked, still getting my bearings.

Mary Ellen answered softly. "A million things could have happened to slow them down. We just got to stay positive. Especially for Bama's sake."

Bama's sake, my ass. I wanted to scream. But I couldn't share my own feelings, the ones I had denied the night before. So I was left alone with my pain, isolated by my lie.

The first day of our exile became a steady stream of increasingly bad news. Worried sick, we switched channels back and forth and listened to reports, hearing one after another about the hardest hit areas of the city. It was like a roll call of my favorite places: Lower Ninth Ward, New Orleans East, Lakeview, and Gentilly.

Midday, the New Orleans security director said that he was sure there had been casualties. "Everybody who had a way out or wanted to get out of the way of this storm was able to. For some who didn't, it was their last night on this earth."

The news got worse and worse. When they confirmed a levee

breach in the Industrial Canal, Mary Ellen let loose a low guttural moan, like something you'd hear in a low budget horror movie.

"It's never the winds that get you in the end. It's always water," Bama said, shaking her head.

We watched real time footage in deadly silence—water pouring into homes, washing them away before our eyes. Six to eight feet, they said, in the Lower Ninth Ward. Bama reached for a hankie in the pocket of her shirtwaist dress, her hand trembling with emotion.

"Oh, dear lord, what if they couldn't get out? My sister can't even swim. She's terrified of water." Bama began to weep.

I allowed myself to consider the unthinkable. What if Antwone and Auntie Shay were still in the Ninth Ward? Underwater. Under siege. On a rooftop. In the attic.

I decided to sweep the fear out of the room. To stay positive, no matter what. Because if we continued to breathe in toxic thoughts and exhale them into the universe, they could gather strength and become real. I grabbed Bama by the shoulders and looked deep into her eyes, like a priest exorcising a demon.

"They left in time. They got out. That much we know for sure. Antwone texted me and told me so."

"What if they turned back?"

"They didn't."

"How do you know that?"

"Because he would have texted me back."

"How do you know?"

"Because that's what we do."

How do you explain cell culture to an eighty-year-old woman who doesn't trust microwave ovens? After a half dozen attempts, Bama became as frustrated with me as I was with her. But at least she stopped crying.

"Okay, Miss Smarty-Pants, then why aren't they here?"

I said maybe he had car trouble; he could be stalled out on the freeway. Bama couldn't remember if he had started with a full tank of gas or not. Auntie Shay had high blood pressure. She could have had an episode, and maybe they had to stop at the hospital. They could be stuck in a hospital emergency room somewhere between here and New Orleans. Or maybe he was so worn out that he had checked into a motel and slept the morning away. Just like me.

"Then why hasn't he called?" Bama said and then added, using my own words against me, "Or texted you. Since that's what you kids do."

Fear crept back into the room.

I had to dispel it. And quick.

"If something bad happened, I would know it. I would feel it in my bones. If last night had been their *last night*, the universe would have clued me in. I would have felt their passing from this side to the other," I said with conviction.

"Why would the universe single you out for some kind of special delivery message?" Bama asked. Although a devout believer in God, she approached the paranormal with grave skepticism.

"My daddy maintains that Darveau women are in touch with the inevitable transition from this life to the other. He told me so himself. We have a natural ability to know the virtual GPS for all the ones we love until that lifeline is severed."

I waited for my mother to say hogwash, which was her usual comment on my daddy's theories on the afterlife. But instead, she said, "Camille's right. That is exactly what Donald would say. I believe that they've been delayed and as soon as he can, Antwone will get in touch with us through more conventional methods."

Jeanette burst into the room with a fresh pot of chicory coffee.

"I just heard on the radio that cell service is all jammed up and they don't have any idea when it will be put right again. No cell with a 504-area code can even receive messages. We were just lucky we got through to Donald before it all went to hell."

We were all reassured for a little bit, but when we still hadn't heard anything by nightfall, we accepted the fact that Antwone had not been able to get out of the city. Perhaps he'd gotten to higher ground. Twenty thousand or so had made it to the Louisiana Superdome, the refuge of last resort. They could be among them.

The next two days passed in a haze. A levee at the Seventeenth Street Canal broke and homes that were spared in the hurricane were now completely underwater as Lake Pontchartrain poured in. The I-10 East bridges were all gone. Eighty percent of New Orleans was flooded and downtown looked like Beirut. The devastation was overwhelming. The wind had torn roofs from houses, snapped telephone poles in half, and ripped two-hundred-year-old oak trees from the ground.

When I saw images of whole neighborhoods turning into lakes, I felt a deep pain in my chest; my heart literally hurt. Like it could crack in two at any minute.

We were breaking down.

Bama took to bed, sick as a dog. Her body could not stand any more bad news. I replayed footage on my laptop of the reports from the Superdome, whose population had grown to 30,000 people, most without food or water. As bad as it looked, I prayed that Antwone and Auntie Shay had made it there. I froze frame after frame, carefully scanning the images, looking for their faces among the sea of refugees.

"I'm going for a walk," I announced late in the afternoon. I had to get out of the house, away from bad news if only for a little while.

"Where to?" my mother asked, attempting a weak protest. She was perfectly comfortable with her teenage daughter roaming around the Quarter unsupervised, but she never felt completely safe in Cajun country.

"Down by the Bayou Teche," I said.

"Well, don't be gone too long. Be back before dark."

I left and closed the door of that bad day behind me.

I made my way through the Port Street Park to the ancient Evangeline Oak, which is named for the heroine in Longfellow's epic poem. According to legend, Evangeline was torn away from her fiancé, Gabriel, during the mass deportation of Acadians from Nova Scotia in the 1700s. After many years of searching for her lover, she finally gave up and joined a convent, brokenhearted. But right before he died, they were reunited under this storied oak tree. Nobody knows for sure if the story is true or not, but folks keep telling it anyway.

Like my daddy, I believed in the power of place, which is why I had come down to the bayou. Great love stories were born out of storms and I felt certain that the tragedy called Katrina would bring Antwone and me even closer together. I sat against the trunk of the Evangeline Oak and, out of habit, stared at my cell. My lifeline was useless to me now. I couldn't get in touch with anyone who mattered. And then it happened. A miracle for sure. My cell actually rang. I answered quickly.

"Hey there, baby girl."

"Is that really you?" I started to cry.

"Who else would I be?" Beano answered.

"Sorry. At first, I thought you were Antwone. He was supposed to be here days ago."

"I know. I talked to your mom. Heard anything heard from Gina?"

"Not since I left. They were staying in town. You know how her mom is about hurricanes."

"I know how her mom is about everything. But they'll make it out just fine. They always do."

"Where are you?"

"Just down the road. In New Iberia. With my evil stepmother and my dad's crazy cousins. I'm having a gay ole Cinderfella kind of time. Seriously, she thinks being gay is a communicable disease that her three-year-old might catch. And my dad won't stand up to her."

"I'm sorry."

"It's okay. I'm dealing with it."

"Nothing seems real anymore, does it?"

"There's more than a breach in the levee. There's a crack in the universe."

"Oh lord, Beano. Don't go getting metaphysical on me. I don't think I can handle it."

"I hear ya. I'm feeling a little unstable myself, which is why I wondered if I could drive over and have dinner with your family."

"You wanna trade in your crazy cousins for mine?"

"Abso-fucking-lutely."

"You familiar with the Evangeline Oak?"

"You're not the only one with Cajun blood. What do you think?"

"When you get to town, swing by the Bayou and pick me up. We'll face the craziness together."

There was a strange silence. I thought I had dropped the call, because Beano never allowed a pause in a conversation.

"Beano? You still there?"

He mumbled a yes. "Antwone's okay. You know that, right? And if I could, I'd trade places with him. So he could tell you so himself."

"You love me that much?" I asked, trying to keep it light.

"I love you both."

I was touched; I knew he meant it. Beano and Antwone had always shared a close connection, maybe because they had both lost their mothers at a young age. I hung up and lay down on the ground. I stared up at the sky through the oak's moss-covered branches, wondering how many girls like me had come to the bayou, dreaming of a reunion with a lost loved one. How many hearts had been broken and how many healed under this tree? I leaned against the trunk of the Evangeline Oak, closed my eyes, and drifted into a waking dream. With every fiber of my soul, I called upon the universe to bring Antwone home.

I don't know how long I dozed, but when I woke up, the sun had begun to set. I looked out over the sun-kissed orangey waters and saw the thin line of day receding into dark. I shuddered so hard it felt like I was having some kind of epileptic fit. As quick as it came, it left. The icy chill was replaced with an eerie calm, a feeling I had never had before.

As I stood, I saw someone walking toward me from the riverbank. The sun was low and in the blinding glare, I couldn't quite make out who it was. I assumed it was Beano, but when he stepped out of the shadows, I realized I was wrong. There was no mistaking that familiar saunter, the sly, almost confused grin on his face. I jumped to my feet and ran to him. I threw my arms around his neck, nearly knocking him over with the weight of my sheer joy. I collapsed my head into his chest and breathed in the aroma of brackish waters emanating from his wet skin, mixed in with the salt of my own tears.

"We were so worried about you. When did you get in?"

"I don't know."

"I bet Bama was so excited to see you. She was wearing herself out with worry."

"I haven't seen Bama. Not since you left 'Orleans."

"Well, didn't you drop Auntie Shay off at the cousins'?"

"I haven't been by the cousins."

"Then where is Auntie Shay?"

"I'm not sure."

"What do you mean? What happened?"

We stood there for a moment, sizing the other up as if we had just met, instead of having shared a lifetime of knowing each other. Then finally, he spoke.

"Where are we? Where is this place?"

"Okay, now you're scaring me."

"Trouble is, I don't remember leaving New Orleans."

"Antwone, you are here. With me. In St. Martinville. At the Bayou Teche."

"I don't know what's happening, but whatever it is, it's crazy bad."

I was frightened for him, because Antwone was never unclear about anything. I sank to the ground. He knelt beside me, wiping away my tears with the back of his hand. I looked up at him and dressed up my voice with reassurance. "Everything is confusing now. But we'll be fine soon as we get back to 'Orleans."

"You can't go home. Not for a long time."

"Oh god, how bad is it?"

"I saw things that I never want to see again."

I reached up and kissed him, long and hard. He didn't fight me, but he didn't exactly kiss me back either. It was as if he was being pulled in different directions.

He leaned against the tree and I curled up his arms, like it was the most natural thing in the world. Only later I would learn that natural had nothing to do with it.

"I want to know what happened. All of it. Start at the beginning."

"With our kiss goodbye?"

I told him yes, because as far as I was concerned, a kiss was always a good place to start.

7.

S itting under a canopy of branches, Antwone told me his story. He began with the chapters I lived, the pre-storm preparations, the decision to leave town, and the phone call from Auntie Shay. But I liked hearing it again from his point of view, especially his take on our first kiss.

"I don't know quite what to make of you, Camille. Or what to do about you. Or with you."

Granted, I would have preferred hearing something more like, "You rock my world," but at least his confusion was a step in the right romantic direction.

Gradually, he eased into the parts of the story I didn't know, the storm's beginnings. He described driving to the Ninth Ward, watching the wind sweep the falling rain from one side of the road to the other as soon as the drops hit pavement. He pulled into the driveway of Auntie Shay's shotgun house with one purpose: get her and those cats out of the city fast.

"But everything took too damn long. When I got there, she had cooped up eight of the cats in the kitchen and was tearing through boxes in the basement, looking for King Oliver.

"She sent me upstairs to crate the kitchen kitties, while she kept looking. It took me half an hour to wrangle seven of 'em and another twenty minutes to find Miss Pearl, who had wedged her big fat kitty self between the wall and the stove. Freeing her took another twenty minutes. After I finished, I begged Auntie Shay to give it up, 'cause I knew if we didn't hit the road soon, we'd be stuck. But she wasn't having any of it."

Antwone tried to reason with his great auntie, telling her that King Oliver had disappeared because he sensed a storm coming. She needed to trust his feline judgment to keep him safe. But Auntie Shay refused to set one foot out of the Ninth Ward until they found him.

"So I struck a deal. I would make one more round of the neighborhood and after that, we would leave with or without King Oliver.

"She agreed and I started out. You can't believe how many people were still left. Folks who had no way of getting out. And they all knew King Oliver. He owned that block. DeShawn Carter's six-year-old niece told me she had seen him around eleven running across the street to avoid being run over by a big semitruck.

"I figured if he could survive the truck, he could survive the storm, so I went back. Auntie Shay was waiting for me on the front porch, ready to go. Overnight bag in one hand, Sunday purse in the other. But when she saw me empty-handed, she marched right back into the house and threw her purse on the sofa. I followed and told her calmly that she had made me a promise. She said her promise was no good, that she had crossed her fingers behind her back.

"I told her to pick up her purse and get her black ass out to my car. I never talked street to her before, but I might as well have gone all gangster for all the good it did. She told me to leave and take the other cats with me. But she wasn't going anywhere until King Oliver came home.

"About that time, DeShawn, who's a couple years older than me and lives down the street, came running into the front yard. He wanted to know if there was room for three more in the car. He wasn't asking for himself but for his sister's kids. Her oldest was the little girl who had seen Oliver and the youngest was just a baby. It was down to the wire. Winds were kicking up. Rain was coming down hard. We didn't have much time before the storm hit for real."

"So you took the kids and left, right?"

"That would have been the smart move, for sure," Antwone

said, half-smiling. "But what I did instead was give DeShawn the keys to my car.

"I couldn't leave Auntie Shay and it didn't seem right to waste a full tank of gas when there was still time to get those kids out. So that's how it went down. We unloaded the cats and strapped in those kids—all the while their mother was crying, thanking and hugging me. You should have seen the look on that little girl's face pressed against the rear window, blowing me kisses as they pulled out of the driveway. There are lots of decisions I made over the last few days that I regret but giving DeShawn the keys to my car ain't one of them."

"Wait a minute," I interrupted him. "If he took your car, then how *did* you get here?"

"That's what I keep telling you. I don't know."

He ran his hands down the leg of his jeans like his body didn't belong to him, like he was puzzling out his own existence. His uncertainty unsettled me.

"After DeShawn left, I boarded up a few windows and then hunkered down in the family room at the back of the house to ride out the storm with Auntie Shay and those damn cats. She sang every hymn she knew. I don't know what was worse—the sound of the wind shaking the windows or the sound of her voice 'cause Auntie Shay can't sing worth shit. Luckily, she wore herself out trying to remember the words to all the verses and went to sleep.

"Winds died down the next morning. And when the sun came through the cracks in the boarded-up windows, Auntie Shay started praising Jesus for delivering us from the storm. I told her to stay put while I checked things out. Before I got to the front door, there was a loud boom, like a bomb going off. Books fell off the shelves. Dishes crashed to the floor. I didn't know which way was up."

"Oh my god, Antwone. That must have been from the levee breaking on Canal Street."

"It was the gates of hell opening up," he said. "I threw open the door to see what was going on. And then—"

Antwone rested his head on his hands. His sigh came from deep within him. I could feel his pain inside my own chest.

"Then what?" I asked.

"The water came."

I leaned into him. The smell of those brackish waters was still present on his clothes, his skin, and in his hair.

"It rushed down the street and swallowed up porches whole. I slammed the door closed and leaned against it like I could stem the tide. Before I knew it, the water was knee-deep. I sloshed back to Auntie Shay, helped her get the crated cats upstairs to the attic, tossed her my cell for safekeeping, and then ran back downstairs. By then the water was waist-high and her house had turned into a swamp. God, it was awful—the stench alone could kill you. And there were snakes in the water. How did that even happen?

"I grabbed cans of food and sodas, anything floating by. When I had all I could carry, I started back upstairs. But I stopped at the locked gun case in the hallway. I could see the top half of Auntie Shay's shotgun above the waterline. I put the canned goods on the step above me, kicked the case with my boot, broke the glass and grabbed up her twelve gauge and a box of ammunition, because you just never know.

"Thank god that by the time I got to the attic, Auntie Shay had calmed down considerably. She let the cats out of their crates, which I thought was a good idea. Whatever happened, they'd have a better chance surviving that mess on their own.

"I dumped the stuff I grabbed from downstairs on the floor and we counted out what I had: four sodas, three cans of beans, one can of pumpkin pie filling, two cans of tomatoes, one bottle of hot sauce, and a tin of sardines. Auntie Shay was disappointed.

"She said she had hoped I had remembered to get some cat food. She said it like I had just got back from the corner store. Air was so heavy I couldn't breathe. I picked up the shotgun and fired into the ceiling, which sent the cats scattering. Auntie

Shay screamed at me to stop shooting up her house. I told her that I was making air holes so we could breathe easier. But the truth was that it felt good to shoot something, even if it was the shitty roof over our heads. She told me to put the gun down and do something more constructive, like call 911 so they could send someone over to rescue us. Two things were wrong with her plan. First, I knew that her all-Black neighborhood was the last place they'd go to help people out. And second, my cell hadn't worked all night. But I also knew better than to argue with her, so I dialed 911 and I'll be damned if I didn't connect to a real person on the other end of the line. I told the operator our address and situation. I said that if the water rose two more feet, we'd need a boat rescue. I gave her landmarks—buildings, trees, our position to the canals—so that the rescue team could find us. I explained that they would have to cut us out because we didn't have a way to get to the roof and my great auntie couldn't swim. She didn't say anything for so long I thought I'd dropped the call. Finally, she spoke up. 'There is no rescue team,' she said, but before she hung up she added she was sorry. Auntie Shay couldn't wait to hear what the woman had to say. I lied and told her that they were going to send help as soon as they could. I mean, what was the point of telling her we were on our own? She was so happy she opened up the can of sardines and fed them to the cats to celebrate. I loaded up the shotgun and blew a couple more holes in the roof. After a little while, Auntie Shay got worried. She was afraid they wouldn't be able to find us since the street signs were probably underwater. I poked around and found an old white dress shirt in a trunk that had belonged to Uncle George. I attached the shirt to the end of his fishing pole and fired another round of shots through the ceiling to create a hole big enough to slip the pole through. And then I raised my homemade white flag, so that the rescue team that *wasn't* coming could find us when they *didn't* get there.

"I can't tell you how long we waited. What little we had to

eat we shared with the damn cats. Auntie Shay got real quiet. I worried about her heart giving out.

"When I could see water coming up through the cracks in the attic floor, I knew it wouldn't be long before the whole house was underwater. I'd like to tell you that I made my peace with dying, but that would be a lie. I started praying hard. Then I started cussing. Then I went back to praying. Back and forth between prayers and profanity, rage building up inside of me.

"I was teetering on the brink of losing it altogether when I heard the sounds of deliverance: the buzzing of a chain saw, followed by a man's voice from above, asking how many of us were in the attic. We hollered back and he told the two of us to move to the north side of the room. We watched as wood and crap fell into the attic, leaving a four-foot hole in the ceiling. We could see the faces of two men—one white and one Black—staring down at us.

"I later learned they were a couple of off-duty cops who were rescuing folks, one boatload at a time, and taking them to higher ground in a twenty-foot fishing boat. They pulled and I pushed and somehow we got Auntie Shay out of the attic and up on the roof. She was scared to death because the winds had picked up. She yelled at me to crate up the kitties, but the Black cop said they weren't no Noah's ark. They only had room for people. She didn't argue with him, which halfway made me mad. How could she put up such a fuss with me and then give in to a complete stranger?

"We somehow got Auntie Shay into the boat, which was not easy. There were four others in it already, an old Black man, his daughter, and twin granddaughters. And we started on our way. When we motored past the Calliope housing project, we saw hundreds of people hanging out of their second-floor windows screaming at us to pick them up. But the white cop said we had to keep going.

"I said that we had room for at least two more, but the Black cop said if we got anywhere near that building, folks would start jumping out like rats on a sinking ship. Half of 'em would die and the other half would take us down with them. I knew he was right, but if I close my eyes, I can still hear them screaming.

"Not too much later, we spotted a family, maybe eight of them altogether, in a leaky fiberglass boat. We threw them a rope and started towing them. And just when we could see the overhead bridge on I-10 up ahead, our boat stopped dead in the water. The motor got so fouled with crap that it locked up. The wind was still blowing hard. While his partner lifted the motor out of the water to clear it, the Black cop held on to a power pole to keep us from crashing into the trees. Auntie Shay started breathing hard, saying she felt like she was having a heart attack or something. 'It's funny, isn't it?' she said. 'Because here I've been terrified that I would die in the water. You just never know. You just never know.'

"But once again, disaster was averted. Auntie Shay calmed down and somehow the two cops got the motor to restart. I helped them lower it into the water. And as we got underway, the folks in the other boat started cheering. They got so excited they capsized the damn thing. Men, women, and children fell into the water. One of them was just a boy, no more than seven. He was flapping his arms like a bird shot out of the sky. It was obvious the kid couldn't swim, so I pulled off my heavy belt and dove in. Water was eight feet deep at least. I managed to grab hold of him when this other woman, crazy scared, climbed on top of me. They forced me underwater and pinned me down—seconds, maybe minutes. Somehow, I pushed my way to the surface long enough to shout, 'You're drowning me.'

"No one heard. Not the two cops who were in the water, fishing people out of it. Not the boy who grabbed me by the neck. Not the woman who pushed me deeper into the water. I struggled, but the weight of their bodies kept pushing me down. After a couple of minutes, I realized I was sinking, like all the air had been sucked out of my body. I started inhaling water and it burned when it went down. I looked up and thought I could see a break at the surface. I tried to swim toward the light, but my arms were too heavy to move. I closed my eyes and let go."

I waited for him to tell me the rest of it, how one of the cops pulled him out of the water into the boat and gave him CPR. But when I asked what happened next, he just stared off into the distance. Finally, I spoke. "All that matters is that you're here now and I love you."

I knew it was too soon to say those words, but I didn't care. I liked the way they sounded when they left my mouth: soft and gooey like warm chocolate brownies straight out of the oven.

"Oh, baby girl, loving me is probably not a good idea."

"I don't care. I love you anyway."

This time the words came out with a steel-like resolve that could withstand high winds and water. He stood up, pulled me to my feet, and laid the back of his hand against my cheek.

"I'm pretty sure I died in the storm."

"That's impossible. How could you have died if you're here with me now?"

"I don't know. I remember hearing Auntie Shay screaming, rocking the boat with her grief. But her voice was soon drowned out by a chorus of others, some familiar and some not, calling out to me as I was pulled into a deep dark tunnel that opened up to—well, I can't really describe it. It was like floating in liquid light. And just when I heard Grandpa Tito's voice crying out Big Chief chants, a strong force sucked me back through the tunnel and landed me here with you."

"I don't want to hear anymore."

"Listen to me, Camille. I'm telling you this so you will know where to find my body, because it will be important to Bama."

I started crying.

He took me by the shoulders. "You remember the I-10 overpass where the Treme meets the Ninth Ward?"

I nodded. I knew the place well. In what seemed a lifetime

ago, the two of us had joined Mardi Gras crowds under those massive concrete pillars to mark the spot where it all began— the brass bands, jazz funerals, and Mardi Gras Indians. We ate crawfish off portable barbecue grills and danced in the fading light of day. And now our dance floor was a river bottom.

"Auntie Shay's on that bridge, and she's gonna die if she doesn't get to hospital. Promise me you'll find a way to get her the help she needs."

First M–. Now Auntie Shay. What kind of superpowers did he think I had?

Just then, there was a loud crash in the church parking lot at the crest of the hill. I looked up to see a two-ton flatbed truck plow into a parked red Hyundai. "Oh my god, that's Beano's car!" I yelled.

All this talk of death and dying caused me to panic. Terrified that I might have lost Beano, too, I ran up the hill to the parking lot. I looked inside the car window expecting to see Beano's mangled body, but the car was empty. The truck driver threw open the cab door and jumped out, skittish as a cat. Beano, who had evidently bailed to find me before the crash, came up from behind me, steadying himself. He leaned over to check out the damage and then turned toward the driver.

"Well, lucky for you, it sounded worse than it is. I got so many dents on this bumper I can't tell which one you caused."

"Then we're good?" the truck driver asked nervously. He smelled like beer.

"We're good," Beano said.

"Wait for me here." Relieved that my best friend was okay, I turned and ran back to the river.

The sun had set and the evening sky was a dusky purple, streaked with wisps of pink. But Antwone was gone, nowhere to be seen, disappeared into thin air.

I felt a startling jolt, like when you wake up from a deep sleep and realize you are in your own bedroom and not being chased down Bourbon Street by drunk monkeys.

When Beano, who was supposed to wait by the car but never did anything I told him to do, approached, I started crying. Seeing how upset I was, he put a comforting arm around my shoulder. I closed my eyes and took in the faint but distinctive scent of Antwone.

"What's wrong, sweetie?"

"He was here. Underneath this tree. With me."

"Who was here?"

"Antwone."

Beano took a careful pause before asking: "If he was here, then where is he now?"

"I don't know. I don't understand any of it myself."

"Camille, you are bordering on crazy talk. You know that, right?"

"All I know is that he was here with me. I heard his voice. I felt his touch. He held me in his arms and told me he had died in the storm."

"Stop right now. 'Cause you are not devout enough to go all Saint Teresa on me, having visions and ecstasies and all that other shit."

He was right about that. And I knew for certain I couldn't tell another living soul what *might* have happened under the Evangeline Oak—not until I figured it out myself.

8.

I didn't say much on the ride back to my cousins'. Had I seen Antwone's ghost? Or had I experienced a waking dream? I couldn't figure it out.

Beano didn't pry. Nor did he comment when we found Mary Ellen sitting zombie-like on the couch in the Darveau family room, surfing the news on my laptop. She hadn't changed her clothes from the day before or showered. I had a hard enough time dealing with my mother when she was in a regular mood but being around her when she was falling apart was just too much.

Her appearance didn't seem to bother Beano, who blew straight past me to the laptop like it was a gift from God. His own had been left behind in the hurry to get out of town and his Cajun cousins didn't even have dial-up that worked properly.

"Whatcha watchin'?" he asked.

She turned the screen to show us both. I stopped cold at the headline of the article she was reading: "Thousands Stranded on the I-10 Overpass in the Ninth Ward."

Just like Antwone said. I studied the blurred photo. Was Auntie Shay waiting on that bridge? I couldn't make out any of the faces in the photo. But if she was among those desperate people who made it through the water and now were waiting to be rescued from the overpass, how could I, hundreds of miles away, help her?

"Have you tried getting in touch with folks through Facebook?" Beano asked.

I was immediately shamed that it had not occurred to me to check on people via the most popular social network in the history of the universe. Mary Ellen handed me the laptop and Beano hovered over my shoulder as I logged into my home page.

"Oh my god, Camille. You only have eleven friends? How is that even possible?"

"Miranda Blake," I answered.

"That skank from eighth grade who gave blowjobs to seniors at halftime and said it wasn't sex?"

"I'm pretending I didn't hear that," Mary Ellen said.

"You've had plenty of time to manage her collateral damage," Beano said, clearly disappointed in me.

"What did she do to you?" Mary Ellen asked.

"After she friended me as a slumber party joke, she said I stalked her."

"You kinda did," Beano noted.

Miranda made it clear to everyone I knew that I was a social networking piranha. In a twenty-four-hour period, I shed Facebook friends like a snake sheds skin.

Since that day, I have logged into my home page approximately three times, once by mistake. It was not surprising to see that in the past week I had missed two very important messages. The first was from Gina, posted not more than eight hours before, saying that her family had survived the storm and the flooding. Trees were down, but the house was still standing.

And I had a friend request from Anita Cocktail.

Mary Ellen started crying. Everything she had held back in these past few days—every worry, every fear—came out in a torrent of tears. And once she started, she couldn't stop.

She read Miz Cocktail's status update over and over again, twice out loud.

"We are alive and well, six of us altogether. Some of the streets in the Quarter have taken on water, and some of the buildings were damaged by wind, but most of the major landmarks, just like us, remain intact. We only have intermittent internet connection, so we get most of our news from a.m.

radio. We have crowned Donald Darveau the unofficial Mayor of Bienville because he has kept our spirits high and our glasses full. And no one tells a better story."

When she read it for the third time, I was seized with inspiration. You know those cartoons when somebody gets an idea and a light bulb appears above their head in the next frame? Well, that's exactly what it felt like. I knew exactly how to get help to Auntie Shay. And all I needed was five minutes alone with my computer.

Which turned out to be near to impossible. After Beano made a "live chat" request to Miz Cocktail, he and Mary Ellen parked themselves in front of the computer for five hours straight. I tried various tactics but couldn't get either one of them to budge. Around midnight, Mary Ellen decided it was too late for Beano to drive home and insisted he spend the night with us.

Jeanette was not pleased. "Mary Ellen, you are family, but I'm not running a bed and breakfast. Where's he gonna sleep?"

"We can make him a pallet on the floor in the bedroom with the girls," my mother answered.

"I don't know how you do things in New Orleans, but I won't allow a boy to sleep in the same room as my precious girls."

"It's okay, Miz Jeanette. Your girls are safe. I'm gay," Beano said, reassuringly.

"Oh lord, lord, lord," Jeanette muttered, leaving the room.

"I'm not sure if you made it better or worse," Mary Ellen told him, and we shared the first laugh of the day.

"Why don't you guys take a break? I'll stay online while you get Beano settled," I offered, hoping to steal a moment alone with the computer.

"I think it'd be better if I slept on the sofa," Beano suggested.

He curled up with a blanket, and I tried to stay up with Mary Ellen. But I must have dozed off in my chair, because around two in the morning, Mary Ellen startled me awake.

"Your daddy's online and I can't figure out how to message him back."

By the time I got to the keyboard, we had dropped the connection.

"What the hell happened?" Mary Ellen asked.

"They must have lost their internet."

"How do we get it back?" My mother was about as technologically savvy as Bama.

"We just have to wait for them to reconnect. Why don't you go make yourself a drink? I'll yell if he comes back online."

Beano was snoring lightly when Mary Ellen left for the kitchen. I could hear the tinkling of ice cubes hitting the glass and knew I had just enough time to send off an email to Miz Cocktail. Mary Ellen was as fastidious as Donald was at making a proper cocktail, but she wasn't as fast. Old Fashioneds were her favorite. She insisted on Maker's Mark bourbon and Angostura bitters. I knew from experience that once the ice hit glass, I had three minutes tops before she returned, drink in hand, stirred to perfection.

I was afraid if I sent Miz Cocktail a Facebook message, Mary Ellen would see it, so I emailed her asking her to tell my father that Auntie Shay was stranded on the I-10 overpass between Treme and the Ninth Ward. I said that I had seen a photo of her on CNN and that she looked like she was in bad shape.

"Promise not to tell the others," I wrote, "because I don't think anyone here can handle one more ounce of worry."

I pressed send and logged back on to the Facebook message board just as Mary Ellen slipped back into the room. Exhausted, I left my mother alone with her cocktail and trudged back to the girls' room. All three cousins were sound asleep. I crawled into the trundle bed and stared at the popcorn ceiling, trying to make sense of the day. What happened under the Evangeline Oak had felt so real, but it surpassed my understanding of how the world of the living connected to the world of the dead. I didn't know whether to look to science or superstition or religion for answers, not being an expert in any of those subjects.

So I prayed to the God I knew to watch over Auntie Shay and

I prayed to the gods I did not know, the ones who controlled the edges of the universe where spirits lurked, to bring Antwone back to me again. I prayed so hard I began to cry. I must have finally cried myself to sleep because the next morning, my eyes were red and swollen and my cousins had once again left for school without waking me.

I stumbled into the kitchen and helped myself to a cup of chicory coffee from the stove. Mary Ellen, who must have had about ten cups already, ambushed me to say she'd finally contacted Donald who told her that he was leaving New Orleans.

"He gave Miz Cocktail his forty-four and posted a sign on the door that said, 'Looters will be shot on sight,' which is an outright lie because the gun isn't loaded. He left the ammunition at the house. He said he was headed for the I-10 because he heard the Red Cross was sending in buses to evacuate people stranded on the overpass."

There it was. He had gotten my message and was going to the flooded part of the city to find Auntie Shay.

Even though I had managed to keep my promise to Antwone, I became paralyzed with worry. In the three days that followed my daddy's announcement that he was leaving New Orleans, I stopped changing my clothes. Sometimes I forgot to bathe, and my hair became a rat's nest of tangles. My mother barely noticed. She was too busy putting on makeup and primping for my daddy's homecoming. She even ventured downtown to buy a new dress.

I no longer even had Beano to keep me company. When he got back to his cousins' home, his stepmother blew up at him for staying the night with us and took away his car keys. He was livid.

"She grounded me, and my dad just sat there and let her. Can you believe that? The woman's completely irrational. Our city is drowning and she 'grounds' me? And here's the best part. She doesn't even see the irony in that."

❧

We knew it would take time for my daddy to get to us. But after four days and no word, we were all getting edgy. That evening, as we were clearing off the supper dishes, we heard a knock at the front door.

"I'll get it," Jeanette said, but Mary Ellen bolted past her like a marathon runner headed for the finish line. We followed and watched as she flung open the door.

Through the screen, we could see my daddy. His face was sunburned, his pants caked with mud. He turned and waved goodbye to the trucker who had given him a ride in his eighteen-wheeler from the bus stop in Lafayette. I strained to see if anybody else was with him, but he was alone. In that moment, I realized how ridiculous I'd been to think he would be able to find Auntie Shay in the disaster that had been our city. I also began to reconsider everything that had happened. In that doubt arose a flutter of hope. Maybe I had dreamed the whole thing. And maybe Antwone was still alive.

Bama, who had quit taking meals with us, emerged from her room just as my daddy stepped across the threshold. We clung to him like he was a lifeline to our former lives, showering his dirty body with hugs and kisses, crowding him with our love and peppering him with questions about how he got out of New Orleans.

"Good lord, Donald, what happened to your shoes?" Mary Ellen asked, noticing he was barefoot.

"Well, I guess I lost 'em. Probably when I was wading through the waters."

"Oh, mon cherie," Jeanette exclaimed. "Can I get you a little something to eat? To drink?"

Donald shook his head.

"I have some news," he said and gestured to Bama to sit with him on the couch. My heart was racing. He cradled Bama's hands in his own, speaking in a voice so gentle it almost sounded like a lullaby.

"I found your sister on the big overpass that connects Treme to the Ninth Ward."

So that much was true.

"She was pretty weak when I got there. She'd been through a lot. And she lasted another three, four hours as we waited for help to come."

"Shay-shay is dead," Bama said quietly.

"I was holding her in my arms when she passed. I want you to know that she did not die alone, that she was with family," he said, as if that were important. And I guess it was to Bama, because she seemed comforted.

"Was she scared?" Bama asked.

"No. She went gently, like a babe going to sleep," he answered.

"What did you do with her body?"

"When the first bus came, I asked the driver if I could bring her with me, but he said no. He could only evacuate a third of those on the bridge as it was. So I gave up my spot on the bus and decided to wait for the next one, in order to take care of your sister."

Trembling with emotion, Bama punctuated his story with mumbled thank-yous.

"There was a patch of dry land on the slope going down to the underpass, so I carried her there and laid her on the damp grass. I found a tarp among the wreckage and covered her, securing it with pieces of broken brick, what was left of somebody's chimney. Then I went back to the bridge and asked if anyone had a pen or something I could write with. Sure enough, halfway across the overpass, I found a kid with a Sharpie. I asked him if I could borrow it for just a minute and promised to bring it right back, but he was reluctant. His cell was gone. He didn't have any water or food or even a flashlight, but he had this one thing—this Sharpie pen—and he didn't wanna let go of the last thing he owned. I promised him that if he would let me use his pen, that on his eighteenth birthday, he could come down to the Quarter and drink for free at my bar.

"He stared at me long and hard. 'How do I know you even own a bar?' he said. 'Well, you don't,' I said. 'But I do and that's the truth.' He said, 'Yeah, well, your deal's only good if you survive this mess. Who knows what's coming next.' I said, 'Whatever it is, I have to survive it, because if I don't, my wife will kill me.'"

Mary Ellen smiled and laid her hand on his shoulder.

"I told the young man that I had made a grave for an old friend, a lady old enough to be his grandmother, who had died on the bridge. And I needed to mark her passing so that when this was all over, her sister could claim the body and give her a proper burial. He walked with me to Auntie Shay's temporary resting place. He still wouldn't let me have his pen, but he agreed to write the epitaph himself. We kept it simple so as not to use much ink. I told him to write, 'Here lies Sharon Williams. Lover of animals. Friend to all.'"

"But what about my Antwone? Why wasn't he there with her?" Bama asked.

The moment of truth had come. I held on to hope like it was real.

Daddy turned to Jeanette. "If you wouldn't mind, could you bring us a bottle and some shot glasses?"

"Donald Darveau, you tell me what happened right now. I don't wanna wait on whiskey," Bama said forcefully.

"Your grandson was a real hero," he began.

And I knew the rest.

Everything he described was just as Antwone had told it to me: beginning with the cats and the storm and its aftermath, being trapped in the attic, Antwone's ingenious use of the white flag to signal their location, the rescue by the off-duty cops, their motor stalling out, and the capsizing of the boat they were towing.

"Auntie Shay said that when Antwone heard the little boy screaming, he was the first to go into the water, even before the cops, who were some kind of heroes in their own right. Your grandson died sacrificing himself for others."

"Oh lord, lord, lord. I have lost them both!" Bama let out

a low, guttural moan that sounded like the plaintive cry of a wounded coyote.

That doublewide living room was awash with tears: Jeanette, my cousins, my mother, and even my father all cried openly—everybody but me. I ran from the room.

There had been times in the last week when I thought the worst was over; nothing worse could happen to me. And then something worse did happen. And then something worse after that until I had become desensitized. My armor had been ripped away to raw nerves that bled inside out. I had no more tears left.

Marguerite followed me to the back of the house into the kitchen.

"If you really loved him, then why aren't you crying? I guess your momma was right about that Black boy not being your boyfriend."

"Fuck you and your racist bullshit, Marguerite. The only *boy* in my daddy's story was the one saved from drowning. The one who saved him was a man."

I slammed the door and stepped into the backyard. My daddy found me some time later, sitting by myself on the tire swing, which hung on the sycamore in the middle of the yard. I was listening to the high-pitched, buzzy birdsong of a warbler perched in the branches above me.

Daddy rubbed my shoulder, and together we took in nature's concert—birds, cicadas, and bullfrogs all chiming in together. "There are no birds left in the Quarter. They're all gone. Dead or flown away. It's strange to walk through the streets in the silence they left behind. There's something I have to ask you, Camille. How did you know I would find Auntie Shay on the overpass?"

"Like I said, I saw her face in a photo on CNN."

"The young man who loaned me his pen said there hadn't been a news team on that bridge for two days."

He knew I had lied. But how could I tell him what had happened when I myself didn't even know for sure?

"If I tell you the truth, it's gonna sound like the biggest lie I've ever told."

"Then you have no choice."

I told him a version of events in a flood of words, how Antwone had appeared to me, how he told me everything that had happened. I did leave out the kissing part for obvious reasons. I was sure my daddy did not want to hear about my sex life, even if it was with a boyfriend who was dead. When I finished, I waited for his reaction, heart in hand. He measured his words as carefully as he did the booze for his signature drinks.

"I am not surprised that he chose you. You are blessed with a natural gift and a receptive heart. Like my own mother, you seem to be able to bridge the waters between this life and the next."

Overwhelmed with relief, I swallowed the doubts that had been worming their way into my consciousness. I badly needed someone to help shape the story, to sift out the fiction from the facts. According to my daddy, who I trusted above all others, I wasn't crazy. I had inherited a gene that made me vulnerable to ghosts and spirits.

"Would it be wrong to try to summon him back?" I asked.

Mary Ellen pushed opened the screen door just in time to hear his answer to my question.

"We have no control over the spirit world. They appear at their will, not ours."

"Don't be filling her head with hogwash," Mary Ellen said. "Ghost stories are just that. *Stories* about ghosts. And ya'll should come in before the mosquitoes eat you up."

My daddy kissed me on the top of my head and whispered, "Best not to mention any of the rest of it to your mother."

Every day for the rest our exile, I returned to the Evangeline Oak, willing Antwone's spirit to reappear. Once, upon waking from a nap, I felt the lingering presence of him, but as soon as I tried to coax him into the real, the feeling disappeared. At some point, I accepted that his first appearance had been a final goodbye, that I would never see him again.

And I began to grieve.

9.

After the evacuation orders were lifted at the end of September, we hugged our relieved cousins goodbye and made our way back to town, not knowing what would be waiting for us when we got there.

What we found was a mess with a capital *M*, including a mountain of bureaucratic red tape that made identifying the dead a monumental task. Our first week back, Daddy drove Bama to traveling morgues set up in tents and trailers all over town to look for the bodies of Antwone and Auntie Shay. While Bama and Daddy searched among the dead, Mary Ellen and I were tasked with assessing the damage to our home. We drove through the once-thriving Lakeshore neighborhood, its sidewalks now lined with broken refrigerators and buildings with huge chunks carved out of them.

We couldn't turn onto our street because the road was completely blocked by a cypress so big it must have been at least a hundred years old, ripped out of the ground by the storm and laid to rest across the road like a dead soldier. We parked the car and hiked the last six blocks on foot.

"Whatever it is, we'll deal with it," my mother said. But neither of us was prepared for what we found when we got there.

As we approached, the first thing I noticed was a gaping, gut-wrenching hole in the roof of Antwone's shotgun house. All that was left of the side porch where he broke up with M— was the old swing half-hanging off its chain.

I looked beyond his wrecked house, searching for my own in a place where it did not exist. It was simply gone. I struggled in my mind to rethink the geography of the place among the boards and bathroom tile and crushed furniture. Remnants of my former life emerged from the rubble, like a museum exhibit documenting a lost civilization. I walked through the relics and discovered Antwone's things were mixed in with mine. A hot pink stiletto poked up from under his senior lettermen's jacket. I left the shoes but took the jacket. My first confirmation dress lay next to his New Orleans Saints baseball cap. It went on and on. A torn shirt, my favorite purse, his sweats, my plastic hairbrush were all tangled up together, our lives twisted in an intimate way they hadn't been before the storm.

"Oh my, the house is gone," Mary Ellen said.

My mother had a real knack for stating the obvious.

"If you're looking for your garage, it's right over here," our neighbor Adele yelled. "Smack dab in the middle of my porch."

And sure enough, our old garage had destroyed what used to be one of the finest rose gardens on our block and come to rest under the eaves of Adele's front porch. It was ironic that the only part of our house still standing had been a sore spot between my parents for some time.

Our detached garage was originally located at the back of our property. Mary Ellen considered it an eyesore and wanted to tear it down, but Daddy thought it added a certain charm to the place. Charm aside, it was not Fort Knox. In the last two years alone, we had been robbed five times. The first time it happened, they stole Daddy's table saw and his fancy-schmancy, variable-speed DeWalt power drill. He was so mad that he bought a bigger lock and strapped it to the garage door. But the thieves broke that lock two weeks later and this time, they stole my grandmother's sewing machine, which thoroughly distressed Mary Ellen, so my daddy went out and bought an even bigger and more expensive burglarproof lock. Two months later, they drilled through that lock, probably using the DeWalt drill they had stolen the first time, and they took my nearly new Schwinn beach cruiser bike.

After that, my daddy just quit locking the garage altogether.

But when he threatened to clear it out completely so there would be nothing left to steal, my mother objected.

"If we take everything out of the garage, they might start breaking into the house instead."

We reached an interesting compromise between the thieves and ourselves, an urban barter arrangement. We kept the locks off the garage and left enough interesting junk inside to keep the thieves happy. It was like operating our own private Goodwill store. We'd clean out the house, put the junk we didn't want in the garage, and they would come by periodically and take it. It was an almost perfect system.

But now there was nothing left to steal.

Adele threw her arm around my mother's shoulder, shook her head, and said, "Would you just look at that?"

My mother shielded her forehead with her hand and gazed at her garage leaning against the banister of Adele's antebellum porch.

"Well, you can't say I never gave you anything," my mother said.

And she and Adele laughed so hard it hurt. And then they cried. And after that, they laughed some more. And when they finished the second round of belly laughs, they started up with the crying again and they sobbed until they fell to their knees, drowning in tears and laughter.

I thought back to the time before Katrina when people could laugh without breaking into tears, and I wondered if it would ever be that way again.

I stood in rubble where my room once was and tried to remember the fragrance of my sweet olive tree or gardenias blooming wildly in the summer heat. All I could smell now was the leftover stench of the storm. I looked down and saw a tin box, glimmering in the soft sunlight. I picked it up and opened it. Inside was a filigreed fleur-de-lis charm on a delicate gold chain. The enclosed card read: "I love you, baby girl. Now and forever, Antwone."

Baby girl. He had promised to get me something sweet for my sixteenth birthday, but this necklace was beyond all my expectations. The flowering lily had always been tied to New Orleans; the Saints even wore it on their football helmets. Antwone knew how much it meant to me. I clasped it around my neck, proof that what M— suspected all along was true: Antwone loved me. As I reveled in the thought, I looked down the opposite end of the street from where we had come and saw Antwone's silver Honda creeping down our garbage-strewn road.

The car slowed to a stop and my mother bristled when she saw a handsome Black stranger step out. Not only was he driving a car that did not belong to him, he was clearly wearing somebody else's clothes because his pants were a little too short and his shirt too big. His hand-me-downs might have come from Texas or Idaho or even California, care packages sent to those who had literally lost the shirts off their backs in the storm. Mary Ellen flew across the street in a rage.

"What the hell are you doing with Antwone's car?" she screamed accusingly.

"He loaned it to me before the storm so I could get my sister's kids out of the city. I've been trying to find him so I could give it back. Him and Auntie Shay. But nobody's got word."

"You must be DeShawn Carter," I said. My mother's jaw dropped. How the hell did I know who he was?

Before she could ask, the scratchy meow of a demanding feline distracted her. The car window rolled down and DeShawn's six-year-old niece peered out at us from the backseat. Stretched across the rear dash was King Oliver, who amused himself by periodically swiping his paw at the little girl's Afro-puffs. DeShawn said they found the missing cat wandering around a deserted warehouse on Canal Street and wanted to return him and the car to their rightful owners.

I fell to my knees and sat cross-legged on the torn-up lawn, head in hands. The irony of King Oliver having survived when Antwone and Auntie Shay had not was almost too much to bear. It took several more minutes for my mother and DeShawn to sort out the whole story, what he knew about Antwone and the storm's beginnings and what she knew about its tragic aftermath.

When DeShawn learned that Antwone had drowned, he broke down and cried in huge, gulping sobs. She took that young man in her arms and rocked him like a baby until he cried himself out. After he composed himself, he handed her the keys to the car and asked if she could give them a lift back to the Seventh Ward where they were living in a FEMA trailer.

Which left one problem. What to do with that damn cat.

"Does your niece want to keep him?" my mother asked.

"Make him go away, Uncle DeShawn. He keeps messing with my hair," she hollered from the back seat.

"Well, I guess that answers that." Mary Ellen paced the length of Antwone's Honda and back again, considering her next move. "We'll take the cat," she said, sounding like a TV judge making her ruling, "and you can keep the car."

I was stunned at my mother's audacity to give away something that clearly did not belong to her, but even more amazed at her offer to take the cat. She was not an animal lover. Far from it. When I was eight, I begged her to let me have a dog, and she flatly refused. So I downsized from a puppy to a hamster. When she said no, I asked, "What about a bird?" When she shot down that possibility, I lobbied for a reptile, a lizard, or a snake. Mary Ellen countered all my arguments with the same response: "I cannot take on the responsibility for another living thing," meaning that I was as much trouble as any one person could handle. Still, I was so desperate to have a pet that when I found a small mouse shivering in the back corner of the garage, crippled from a near fatal encounter with a predator of some sort, I snuck the poor little thing into my room, made a bed out of a shoebox, and attempted to nurse the tiny little thing back to health.

I failed. I buried any dream of pet ownership the day I buried that mouse.

Even during the years I was obsessed with owning a pet, I had never asked for a cat. I didn't really like them. But before I could object, King Oliver crawled out of the car window and into my lap. Nestled in the crook of my arm, he began to purr contentedly. You could say that from that day forward, the cat was mine. But it'd be more accurate to say that I belonged to the cat.

"Where are we gonna stay?" I asked Mary Ellen on the drive back to the Quarter. "Now that we have a cat, I suppose a hotel's out of the question."

"For now, we'll camp out in the apartment behind the bar. Our tenant is visiting friends in California."

"What will we do when he gets back?"

"One day at a time, Camille. One day at a time," she said as she turned the corner onto our new life.

We moved into the cramped quarters behind the bar. Luckily for us, the architect who rented the tiny two-bedroom apartment called a couple of weeks later from Los Angeles to say that he was trading in tropical storms for earthquakes. My daddy didn't even ask for the back rent, because, frankly, we needed a place to live while we sorted out the insurance and decided whether to rebuild. We boxed up his belongings, shipped them to L.A., and settled into our new, temporary lives.

My high school, demolished by the storm, re-opened in a series of FEMA trailers, which stunk like the science lab on frog-dissection day. The administration was forced to strip away our school programs: sports programs were cancelled because there were no fields or gym; the theater department evaporated because there was no stage; no more orchestra because the instruments were lost in the flood. All that remained were core academic classes and the smell of formaldehyde. That was the worst part. That and the fact that Beano was held prisoner in New Iberia.

His grandmother's stately home on the Esplanade had

survived, but his dad's house was condemned because of water damage. Paranoid about looters and food shortages, his father decided his blended family would stay in New Iberia for the time being.

"My dad sees this as an opportunity for us to become a real family, which is not going to happen until they come up with a cure for my stepmom's homophobia," he told me over the phone. "I amuse myself by teaching my three-year-old brother, Kemper, show tunes just to spite her. You should have seen her face when he belted out 'I enjoy being a girl.'"

"Where are you going to school?" I asked.

"Dad made me enroll in *public* school, because they have a stellar football team. And I'm trying to decide if I should try out for the fall play."

"At least they still have a theater department," I said, trying to cheer him up.

"They're doing *Cats*. And they're going to ruin it," Beano said flatly.

"How can you ruin *Cats*?"

"By setting it in a swamp instead of a junkyard. Our drama teacher thinks turning Rum Tum Tugger into a 'gator will quote, 'enhance the inherent conflict in the play,' end quote."

"You're right. They're going to ruin it."

With Beano in exile, I spent most of my afternoons hanging out with King Oliver. Bama moved in with a widow lady from her church who had an extra room and was thrilled to have the company. Gina was strangely unavailable. Having always been the bad girl, the one voted most likely to get into trouble, she transformed into a rah-rah, let's-put-our life-back-together cheerleader. She became oddly connected to school in a way she never had been before the storm. Second day back, she had lunch with the president of the student body and her do-good cronies. On Wednesday, she joined the school newspaper staff. The very next day, she dyed her hair back to a normal color. By the end of the week, I hardly recognized the girl.

I spent my afternoons grieving, curled up with King Oliver in an overstuffed chair overlooking our little window to the world: a tiny patio garden between the bar and apartment, its once lush foliage ravaged by the storm. I knew my parents were worried about me. I saw concern in their faces. I sensed anxiety in their hushed voices and overheard snippets of conversation.

When Mary Ellen found me for the fourth day in a row curled up with the cat, staring out the window into nothingness, she finally exploded. "You have to get out of your room, Camille. Do something. Anything."

"I am doing something. I'm looking out my window," I answered. "So just leave me alone so I can get back to it."

"You can't hide yourself away forever. It's just not healthy. If you lock yourself away in your bedroom, you will end up just like my father and I won't let that happen."

Great. Just what I needed. Another cautionary tale from Granddaddy's life. Even though I never knew him because he died before I was born, I felt deeply sorry for my mother's father because he never came out well in family stories.

Ignoring my obvious disinterest, Mary Ellen continued: "He was full of potential, but he got drafted and off he went to Vietnam. I'm sure what he saw was horrible and what he was forced to do was unbearable. But other men saw those things and did those things and somehow survived it. But not my daddy. When he came home, his life stopped. Vietnam became his story. He never moved on. He never got past it. He held on to his tragedy like it was something precious worth saving. And the same holds true for you. And everybody else who has ever lived through a disaster. You can move past it. Or you can let it determine the rest of your life. It's a choice you make."

"Well, right now, I choose to look out this window," I said, and she left the room.

❧

The storm changed me for sure, but it did nothing to improve my math skills. After receiving a near-failing grade on an algebra quiz, I resumed my tutoring sessions with my favorite drag queen. The two of us noted a change in the clientele at the Cock's Comb. Many of the regulars had disappeared from the Quarter. Stuck in Houston. Moved to Florida. As late afternoon rolled into evening, new faces emerged among the familiar ones, many of them workers who poured into the city to "help rebuild." Some came out of the goodness of their hearts. Others came just to get work, because there was plenty to be had. But there were those who came because they smelled a buck in the debris and hoped to make a killing off the misfortune of others.

Among the latter was a thirty-year-old Cajun ironworker from Lafayette. His name was Miller McGee. He smelled like cigarettes and always wore a Resident Evil baseball cap, which Miz Cocktail took as a sure sign of his character. Although McGee was a recent transplant himself, he liked to belittle other outsiders scrambling for work.

"I tell you what, ma petite cherie," he said, saddling up to the bar next to me. "Those *Mesicans* sneaking their brown butts in here from Texas—they are the real enemy. Mark my words. Before long, they'll have us eating tacos instead of po'boys and singing 'La Cucaracha' instead of 'Hey Pocky A-Way.'"

"I like tacos," I said defiantly. And I did not like him.

"What makes you so different?" Miz Cocktail asked, closing the math textbook. She had little to no patience for the new wave of carpetbaggers, even the well-meaning ones.

"It's a matter of my lineage," the Cajun answered, flashing a wide grin. His teeth were crooked and discolored. "McGee, that's a French name."

"Sounds Irish to me," commented Old Joe, a kick-ass saxophonist who was well into his eighties but still sat in sessions with all the greats, including Dr. John.

"Bullshit," he said. "I don't know anyone named McGee who don't speak French."

The conversation escalated from there and turned into a

shouting match between Miz Cocktail, Old Joe, and McGee. There were five other patrons sitting at the bar, two of them women. And from time to time, they would add their two cents' worth about McGee's birthright.

My daddy ran a proper, civilized bar where drag queens could comfortably rub shoulders with white-gloved old ladies sipping Long Island iced teas. He was worse than the nuns at school when it came to language. Hate speech of any kind was not allowed and use of the F-word, the N-word, and the C-word was strictly prohibited.

When McGee managed to use all three in the same sentence, my daddy slammed his fist on the bar.

"You, my French friend, are no longer welcome here," my daddy told him.

The other patrons cheered their approval as Daddy grabbed one arm and Miz Cocktail the other and they dragged McGee out the door of the bar.

When they didn't return after a couple of minutes, I got worried and started outside to see what was holding them up. Before I got to the door, Miz Cocktail stumbled back in, blood gushing from her forehead. "Call the police, Camille, before that crazy Cajun kills your daddy."

I tossed my cell to Old Joe and told him to make the call. Despite the protests that I should stay out of it, I rushed out of the Cock's Comb to find my daddy in the gutter tangled up with McGee—fists flying. I grabbed McGee's leg, which gave my daddy a momentary advantage. He rolled the younger man over and pinned his shoulders to the ground. I grabbed his legs to help hold him down. We were all breathing heavy.

"Get off of me," he snarled.

"I'll let you up, if you swear you'll walk down that street and never look back," my daddy said.

McGee bared his teeth like a wild animal. "I swear," he promised and went limp as a bird trapped under a blanket.

"I think we should wait for the cops to get here," I said.

"He gave me his word. If he's the McGee he claims to be, he'll honor his oath."

Daddy rolled off him and McGee lumbered to his feet. I was scared he would come at us again. But instead, McGee dusted off his pants, turned, and walked down the street, just like he had promised.

And that's when I saw it.

A flash of steel shimmering under the soft gaslight on the corner.

McGee whipped around, holding a seven-inch blade. He sliced it through the air at Daddy.

"You are not the boss of me. You ain't gonna tell me where I can and cannot go."

"Walk away, McGee. Before somebody gets hurt," Daddy said, standing his ground.

"Somebody, my ass. I'm the one holding the knife," McGee sneered.

"Forget it, Daddy," I pleaded. "Let's go back inside."

"You best listen to your daughter," McGee snarled. "She's a pretty little thing. I wouldn't mind doing bad things with her."

That did it. Knife or no knife, Daddy shifted his shoulder down like a lineman and head-butted McGee, knocking him to the ground. The knife flew out of his hand, skittering across the pavement into darkness. The two of them rolled around on the sidewalk, punching each other. It wasn't all choreographed like what you see in movies; it was just plain messy. I tried to grab McGee's legs again, but he kicked me in the gut and sent me sailing against the wall.

Just then, Mary Ellen slammed out of the bar, took one look at my daddy wrestling with McGee, and at the top of her lungs, screamed loud enough to be heard uptown, downtown, riverside, and lakeside to boot. We might have waited all night for help from Old Joe's emergency call to 911. But about three seconds after my mother opened her mouth, two policemen, one on horseback, the other on foot, skidded up in time to see

McGee pummeling Daddy with his bloody fist. Neither cop seemed too upset by all the commotion; they took it in stride. The foot patrolman jerked McGee off my daddy and the cop on horseback casually asked, "Somebody wanna tell me what's goin' on here?"

Daddy brushed himself off and explained the situation, followed by McGee's account of events. Nobody mentioned the knife. But I was not about to let that go.

"That man pulled a knife on my daddy," I said. Street fights were one thing, but you do not threaten someone with a knife, not even in the Quarter.

"I did no such thing," McGee hissed. "That little girl's got a big imagination."

That was the first true thing McGee had said all night. I did have a big imagination, but I knew what I saw and what I saw was a big ol' knife. I strained to remember the fight. Did he kick the knife into the gutter? Did it boomerang into the alley? The two cops made a cursory sweep of the street and his person and, finding no weapon, they let McGee go, saying that it might be better for everyone involved if he found someplace else to drink.

The next morning, on my way to the bus stop, I found that knife by accident. Or it would be more correct to say King Oliver came across the blade as he pawed his way under a sack of garbage next to a dumpster, trying to retrieve a half-empty can of albacore tuna. I pulled it out of the debris and considered my options. I could fetch my daddy from the bar and let him deal with it. I could call the police back and maybe they'd arrest McGee. But then the police had a lot on their plate after the storm. Who knows if they'd even filed a report after they broke up the bar fight? There were no guarantees. In retrospect, what I should have done was just throw the knife away. But I didn't.

Traffic in the Quarter was just starting to pick up, so rather than risk being discovered, I slipped the knife into my backpack and on my way to the bedroom, I explained to Mary Ellen that I had forgotten an important homework assignment.

I closed the door and quickly logged onto the internet where I learned that what I held was indeed a military fighting knife: a full-sized, United States-issued Marine Corps knife with a fixed plain edge. You don't use a knife like that to peel an apple or pry open a can. That knife was meant for one thing: killing people at close range.

After all that thinking about what to do, I can't tell you why I did what I did. But I decided to keep it. And just like I had done with that injured mouse, I put it in an empty shoebox and hid it under my bed.

10.

The second week in October, we found Auntie Shay. Her body was so badly decomposed, the coroner had to identify her through dental records. That very day, Bama bought a spiral notebook with a photograph of a cat on the cover and focused all her energies on putting together her sister's life celebration.

Bama became funeral-obsessed; that, we understood. Planning meals, parties, and funerals is a high priority in the Crescent City. Mary Ellen swore she knew people who spent more time planning their own funerals than they did their weddings. But what was troubling was that once Bama found Auntie Shay, she stopped looking for Antwone altogether. Donald took on that responsibility and every afternoon, Mary Ellen would bartend for a couple of hours while he visited and revisited morgue after temporary morgue with no luck and no leads. Antwone's body was lost in the remains of our great city.

One afternoon, after a particularly productive funeral planning session where we discussed whether singing "Down by the Riverside" with all its watery imagery would be appropriate or just plain sad, I gathered the courage to ask Bama if she had given much thought to Antwone's funeral.

"There won't be one," she said.

"What? Why?" I was stunned.

"I'm not so sure he's dead. We haven't found a body."

"But Auntie Shay said—"

"Maybe she got it wrong. Maybe they left him in the water 'cause they thought he was dead. And maybe he somehow made it to higher ground. He was a strong swimmer."

As much as I wanted to believe Antwone was still among us, it didn't make sense. And I couldn't use his ghostly visitation as evidence either. It just wasn't scientific.

"And another thing," Bama said, leaning across the table toward me. "If Antwone had made his way to heaven, why do I still feel his presence?"

"Where do you think he is? Having a beer somewhere in Texas?" I asked, frustrated.

"That's enough, Camille," Mary Ellen said, interrupting with a pot of hot tea that she placed on the table. "Let's just drop the subject altogether."

Which is what we did that day and for many days after. Bama continued to refuse to search for his body, and my daddy kept looking on her behalf. She would say, "When he's ready, he'll come home. Just like that damn cat."

I think that Bama knew her grandson died in the storm, but she wasn't ready to face the truth of his passing. The rest of us steered clear of that conversation, which was unhealthy for starters and terribly unfair, especially to Antwone. How could he be remembered if no one could even bear to speak his name?

In the deep dark of night, I was plagued with troubling nightmares where I saw him trapped in the attic, drowning in the putrid waters, sinking to the bottom of the hurricane-made lake. I would wake in a sweat, terrified and lonely. And there was no one to comfort me. No one but the cat they called King.

On Saturday morning, as I was dressing for Auntie Shay's funeral, my daddy banged on my bedroom door.

"Come on down to the bar, Camille. Somebody's waiting to see you."

I zipped up my little black dress and plowed past him down the stairs, through the courtyard, and into the bar. There amid the early morning crowd was Beano, back from the bayou and looking the worse for wear.

"Oh my god, what happened to your face?"

"This," he said, framing his bruised jaw and blackened eye, "was my ticket back to town."

"Tell me what happened. I know there's a story, and I imagine it's a good one," I said as some of the regulars, including Miz Cocktail, gathered around to hear.

"The usual bullshit. I got the lead in *Cats*. No surprise. They decided to start me as quarterback. Somewhat surprising. But everything was fine until the week my grandmother flew in to see our first game. That Thursday, after practice, a few of the players started mouthing off about how I better not start hitting on them. As if. I like my boys bright and they were all a few bricks short of a load. The smartest one of the group—the one who could actually form words into sentences—cornered me in the locker room, wearing nothing but a jock strap, and accused me of staring at his package. I told him that his *package* was hardly worth a second glance."

"My, my, my," Miz Cocktail said, sipping on her Virgin Mary.

"They got the better of me right quick. He pushed me to the ground and two of his buddies started kicking me in my face and ribs. About eight others looked on. Nobody lifted a finger to stop it. If the coach hadn't come in and broke it up when he did, they might have killed me."

"As happy as I am to have you home, it's just plain sad that it took a hate crime to do it."

"Actually, it wasn't the beating itself. It was what happened afterwards."

"Just like Katrina," Miz Cocktail noted. "It wasn't the storm that got us. It was the water. Beano, my dear, I believe you are a metaphor for our city."

"Thank you. I've always wanted to be one."

"What happened next?" I asked.

"Well, the guys who beat me up were given mandatory detention for two days. But they were still eligible to play on Friday night. Although my father was boiling mad, he thought it best to let it go. But not Grammie. She marched into that principal's office and demanded to know how come those bullies got off so easy. The principal explained that his hands were tied because the school didn't have a policy that protected students from being bullied if they were gay.

"'What if he'd been beaten up because he was Black?' my grandmother asked. 'Oh, the players would have been expelled,' the principal told her. 'What if they had beat up a woman?' she said. 'Oh, they'd definitely be gone on that account,' he said. 'And if my grandson was Jewish?' 'Out,' he said. 'We do not tolerate bullying based on sex, race, color, national origin, religion, or disability. It's all right there in the school policy handbook.' My grandmother leaned across the desk, getting right up in his face. 'Are you telling me that if Beano had been beaten up because he was Polish, those homophobic bullies would have been kicked out of school for the entire year?' 'Yes,' the principal said, 'because being Polish would fall under the national origin clause.' Well, that did it. My grandmother stood up and told that principal that he could shove his inadequate school policy up his ass. She pulled me out of school that very day. And here I am—home free at last."

After he finished his story, we barely had enough time for him to get changed for Auntie Shay's funeral. He borrowed a tie and shirt from my daddy and off we went, running through the Quarter to get to the church. We bumped into Gina in the foyer, who was also fashionably late to the service. At first, we didn't even recognize her; we had no idea, in fact, that she was a natural strawberry blonde.

We slipped into the pew just as the choir began to sing "Nearer My God to Thee." The service itself lasted over three hours. Auntie Shay's preacher had a way with words and used twice as many as necessary. I almost nodded off twice, but Beano was so homesick for 'Orleans that even a two-hour sermon couldn't put him off. And when the brass band played us out of the church, he knew he was truly home.

The steely musicians led our small crowd of mourners across

Basin Street to the City of the Dead. We entered the gates of the cemetery, blinded by the sun-bleached tombs, which looked like miniature houses surrounded by decorative fences of rusty ironwork. In New Orleans, we bury bodies above the ground in family crypts because after a heavy rainfall, the rising water table can literally pop the airtight coffins out of the ground. The walkway was so narrow we had to file through two abreast.

Beano and I passed by the Glapion family crypt where Marie Laveau, the most famous voodoo queen in all of Louisiana, was buried. Small sacrifices were scattered across her grave—curled and dried chicken feet, rooster combs, half-drunk hurricane glasses, cigars, prayers written on paper, and panties.

"Why would you leave your underwear on a voodoo queen's grave?" Beano asked.

"I don't know. Ask my mother," Gina quipped. "I'm sure she's offered up a pair or two over the years."

"That's ridiculous," Mary Ellen said, offering her own opinion on the prayer-embossed thong. "I'll tell you what kind of person leaves their panties on a voodoo queen's grave. The kind who refuses to accept their lot in life, the kind who wishes for more cards instead of playing the hand they're dealt. The kind who is so desperate to hang on to the past, they get caught up in the crazy. Only a fool would do such a thing. And, Gina, your mother is many things, but she is no fool."

After the graveside service, we danced our way back to the Cock's Comb with the brass band. Donald opened the bar for the reception. Earlier, the church ladies from Auntie Shay's congregation had brought over enough food to feed an army, which was a good thing because that's exactly what poured into the bar to pay their respects.

A couple hours later as the crowd began to thin, one last mourner came through the door, just back from Texas and beautiful as ever, the elusive M–. She looked a bit thinner, which suited her. M– was one of those girls who always looked good no matter what they wore or what they weighed or whether their hair was freshly styled or a nappy mess. I hated her so much.

Bama, who held it together during the whole service, broke down at the sight of Antwone's old girlfriend. Her knees buckled; she would have collapsed if my daddy hadn't bolstered her up until she could regain her footing. M— flew to her, and the two women sobbed in each other's arms. The mood sobered and even the lively music from the brass band couldn't turn it back around. Our collective thoughts went from the one we had buried to the one we had not. The one still missing.

"Let's get out of here," Beano said, grabbing my arm.

I agreed and left to change out of my funeral clothes. The last thing I wanted to do that day was deal with M—.

But deal with her I did.

Because when I bounded down the apartment stairs in jeans and a flannel shirt, she was waiting for me on a bench in the empty courtyard, King Oliver curled up in her lap.

"I see you're taking good care of Auntie Shay's cat," she said, scratching him behind the ears.

"He's my cat now and he doesn't really like anybody else holding him but me."

Which was about the stupidest thing I've ever said, seeing as how you could hear King Oliver's loud purrs of contentment two zip codes away. M— continued to pet the kitty as she filled me in on her own post-Katrina journey to Houston and back. Like us, her family stayed with relatives until they could stay no more.

"I'm coming back to St. Bede's in a week," she said. "I need some time. I only just found out Antwone was missing."

I don't know why I bothered but I felt compelled to set her straight. "Antwone died in the storm. My daddy—"

"Bama says your daddy tells stories," M— said sharply.

It was hard to argue with that since Donald was well known for his tall tales. But this was not one of them; I urged her to face the truth. Her lower lip began to tremble, but she did not cry.

"I can't believe I've lost him," M– said.

I'm not very proud of what I said next. I turned mean. "You lost him when he was still alive. You were the one who broke up with *him*."

"How do you know that?" M– asked. "Oh, that's right. You were listening in from your window, weren't you? But what you don't know is that I wasn't going to stay broke up. I was just trying to teach him a lesson. Instead, I broke his heart."

"Well, what *you* don't know is that before he died, he had moved on. He was over you."

"Is that so? Who had he moved on to? You? Girlfriend, let me tell you something. That was never gonna happen. 'Cause he's a strong Black man with a sense of responsibility to *his* people."

"I am his people. We grew up together. Side by side. Shared the same table. Same school. Same parties. Same everything."

"That's a nice white way of seeing the world, Camille."

"I get it. But just because I'll never understand what it means to be Black—"

"Damn straight. And you shouldn't waste time trying. You wanna do something constructive? Think about what it means to be white, to take all that privilege for granted. Don't dwell on what is taken from us on a daily basis but think about what has been given to you without asking. Sit on that awhile."

"What Antwone and I had went beyond the politics of color."

She studied me and when it looked as if her hard exterior might crack, she turned icy cold and scooted the cat off her lap.

"I think you want him to be dead, Camille, because if he's dead then you can take some kind of ownership of him. A kind you'll never have if he's alive and among the missing. As long as he lives and breathes, he belongs to me."

I tried to think of a clever comeback to throw at her, but I came up empty. My hands began to sweat.

"Everything okay out here?" Beano stepped out into the patio, interrupting.

"Just dandy," I said, gritting my teeth. Truth was I had never been so glad to see someone in my life. I couldn't wait to get away from her, and Beano provided the perfect out. We made our excuses, grabbed up Gina who was waiting at the bar, and headed for Café Du Monde. We ordered café au lait and beignets. But even French-style doughnuts smothered in powdered sugar couldn't take away the sting of M—'s words.

The day was unnaturally warm, feeling more like summer than fall. On impulse, I suggested that we go skinny-dipping off the banks of the Mississippi. I knew a secluded spot several blocks away with an easy entry. Gina immediately dissed the idea because now that she had normal hair, she didn't like messing it up. Gina jumped tables to talk to the editor of our school newspaper about writing a column on indie rock bands, and Beano reluctantly agreed to go with me.

We walked through the reeds in silence until we reached my secret place in the Woldenberg Riverfront Park. Although Katrina had damaged the once lush landscape, it had not affected the view of twilight dancing across the Mighty Mississippi. I breathed in the crescent-shaped riverbank like it was oxygen, but Beano viewed the waters with trepidation.

"I don't think we should go in. The current looks strong."

"Chicken-shit," I teased, unbuttoning my shirt.

I gazed at the river. Beano was right; swimming in it was not entirely safe. As I wiggled out of my jeans, I decided to keep on my bra and panties. Not because of what Beano might see but because of what Mary Ellen might say. Just imagine her reaction if they found her daughter drowned *and* naked in the Mississippi River.

I willed the waters to wash away my longing, to bring me closer to the memory of Antwone. As I neared the river, I let my shirt slide off my shoulder and was slammed with the weirdest feeling, acutely aware of my near nakedness, like Eve in the Garden of Eden after she bit the apple. As I stepped into the cool water, I felt a shudder, similar to the one I had felt at the

Evangeline Oak, pass through me. I was so startled that I lost my footing and slipped in the mud, but before I hit the ground, an arm reached out and steadied me with a warning.

"Don't you dare, baby girl."

It was the exact same sentiment Beano had voiced earlier, but it was not his voice that I heard. I slipped the unbuttoned shirt back on my shoulder and turned around.

I saw him. Real. Alive. His beautiful face glistening in the late afternoon sun. I buried my head into Antwone's chest, breathing in his wet skin.

"Whatcha doin'? Taking a chance like that with the waters?"

"I wanted to feel close to you."

"By getting your own self drowned?" He sounded almost angry.

"I was just so sad, because we buried Auntie Shay today."

"I know."

"You do? How? Are you looking down from heaven somewhere, watching us make a mess of things?"

"No, it's not like that."

"What is it like? Where have you been since I saw you last?"

"Back in the tunnel. A deep dark nothingness. Alone with my thoughts. But I know things I have no way of knowing. I feel the life that I'm no longer a part of flying past me."

"Are you in purgatory?"

"Hell, if I know. It's not like there's a street sign identifying the place, but wherever it is, I feel pulled in two directions—to the world and people I used to know and to something beyond, of which I know nothing."

I wasn't ready to admit to him or myself that maybe it was me calling him back from the beyond. "Have you considered that maybe God has a part in all of this? Maybe you're here to serve a higher purpose."

"Bullshit. What would that be? Saving Auntie Shay? 'Cause that didn't work out so well."

I won't lie. I was a little miffed that he didn't seem willing to take any responsibility for his return to earth, so I posed another theory.

"My daddy believes that spirits appear at will."

"Is that what I am? A spirit? A ghost?"

"You feel real enough to me. Okay, consider this. Maybe what's going on is that somebody needs you. And you can't move on until that person doesn't need you anymore."

I looked deep into his eyes, hoping that he would realize that the person who needed him the most was not Auntie Shay or Bama.

"Have you seen M–? Or talked to her? Is she all right?"

How could he be thinking about M– when he was holding a half-naked me in his arms? I could feel his attraction literally rising and pressing against me. My nipples hardened against his wet chest; there was a stirring inside me that longed for release. Ghost. Spirit. Walking dead. I didn't care what kind of magic he was; I loved him more than ever. But I didn't say any of that out loud because if you think you have to be careful about what you say to a live boyfriend, it goes double for a dead one. What I said instead was, "Maybe the someone who needs you is me."

I reached up and kissed him hard. He did not shy away. His lips melded into mine and his hands cupped my butt as he drew me closer. I clenched my eyes shut, trying to hold back my tears, but there was a breach in the levee of my emotions, and I soaked his T-shirt from the outside in.

"Okay, this is weird!" Gina yelled from the shore. Startled by her voice, I opened my eyes and found myself embracing not Antwone but Beano, who was as confused as I was. He pulled away abruptly, his eyes darting back and forth searching for an explanation. Tongue-tied, he hemmed and hawed his way up the riverbank.

"I gotta go. I have this thing I have to do. This important thing. That I have to do. I'll see you later."

When he reached the crest of the hill, he turned and said in parting, "Whatever you think you saw, Gina, you did not. And whatever you think we did, Camille, we did not. We will never speak of this thing that did not happen again. Are we clear?"

"Perfectly," Gina and I said in unison.

"Fine then," he said, adjusting his package, the way guys sometimes do. Even at a distance, I could not help but notice Beano had an enormous hard-on. Gina noticed it too. We all noticed. It was hard to ignore.

"You are really messed up, Camille," Gina said on the bus ride back to the Garden District. "First, you go after a guy who isn't in the game, and now you go after a guy who's not even playing in our ballpark."

"That's not what happened," I said.

I turned my attention to the cityscape whizzing by outside the bus window and pondered this last visitation. Was my gay friend the host body for my dead boyfriend's spirit?

"I know what I saw: you, half-naked, kissing him. And he was kissing you back."

"He was, wasn't he?"

"If you have to ask, then you are even more screwed up than I thought," Gina said.

"I don't think we should talk about it."

"And that would be because why?"

"We promised Beano we wouldn't," I said.

The Betsy greeted us from the kitchen as Gina and I barreled through the backdoor. Still miffed at me, Gina scooted upstairs to change out of her funeral clothes, but instead of following her, I turned toward the kitchen where her mother was heating up milk for coffee on her eight-burner stove. I knew The Betsy would take my questions about the spirit world more seriously than her daughter. She was a true believer. So was my daddy, but I didn't want to discuss my love life with him. There are not many cities in the world where you can sit at the kitchen table, drinking chicory coffee with warm milk, and query your best friend's mother about the spirit world. Thank god, New Orleans is one of those cities.

Perched on a barstool at the old oak table, I bombarded her with questions. Can the recently departed enter a living person's body? How did they do it? And why? Did spirits just hang around on a whim or did they revisit the living with a purpose?

"I need to know how the spirit world works," I said, summing it up.

The Betsy stirred her café au lait with a sterling silver spoon.

"Anyone who tells you they know that is lying, because the very existence of another plane poses more questions than answers. But what I need to know is why *these* questions all of a sudden? Has *somebody* been visiting you?"

"No, but would it be possible, *hypothetically*, for the spirit of someone I lost in the storm to enter the body of my best friend?"

"Oh god, not Gina," The Betsy interrupted.

"Oh no. Not Gina. Of course, not Gina."

"But isn't she your best friend?" The Betsy asked.

"Of course, but this is a hypothetical. So, for the sake of argument, let's say my best friend is Beano. If a spirit entered his body, would he be aware that he was the host?"

"Probably not. Although he might experience residual side effects like vertigo or nausea," The Betsy said, taking a sip of café.

"Well, let's say—and again this is a hypothetical—can the living call back the dead even if the host is unwilling?"

"The answer to that is above my pay grade. You should take your request to a higher authority."

"God?"

"Heavens no. I was referring to the Queen of the Spirit World, Marie Laveau."

"The dead voodoo queen?"

"Who better to assist you? Hypothetically."

She finished her coffee and left me alone with the sinking feeling that I might not ever fully understand how this world works, much less the one beyond. All I knew for certain was that my life had gotten a lot more complicated.

11.

Beano's in love," Gina reported as we ate lunch together on one of six picnic tables scattered outside the row of FEMA trailers. For five days after the incident on the riverbank, Beano had managed to avoid me. Evidently, he had also managed to fall in love.

"Love isn't really Beano's thing," I said, because Beano swore that he was "relationship-saving-himself" for college.

"See for yourself," Gina shrugged, gesturing to our friend walking with Lewis Sinclair, a sophomore from Lakeshore. They were holding hands, their fingers intertwined in an expression of ownership, as if to say, "This is my person. We are together."

"I didn't even know Lewis was gay," I said.

"How could you not? He won the school trivia contest, because he knew that Eleanor Parker was the actress who played the baroness in the film version of *Sound of Music*," she said. "Plus, he absolutely worships Patti Smith."

Gina's gaydar is impeccable.

I watched the two young men, heads together in whispered intimacies. I was so jealous I wanted to cry. The host body for my boyfriend had complicated everything by falling in love himself. I worried that his feelings for another could make him more resistant to Antwone taking over. I knew I was being selfish, but I couldn't help myself. Beano was just flirting with the idea of love. I was committed to it.

I marched over to the table and demanded to talk to Beano—alone. He sucked in air like a diver about to go deep into uncharted waters and asked for Lewis to wait while he "dealt" with me.

As we walked away from the tables of cliques, I explained what really happened at Bayou Teche and at the river. As I told the story, I could see Beano waffling, torn between laws of this world and visions of the other. He recalled our embrace in the reeds.

"It was like I blacked out, like when you're really drunk. And when I woke, all that was left were feelings, not memories."

"And an enormous hard-on," I added.

"We agreed not to bring that up again. Pun intended," Beano said as he paced. "Look, I don't want to be a pod for ghosts. What if other beings start entering my body?"

"Don't be such a drama queen," I chided.

"I can't help it. I am a drama queen. Literally."

"Touché."

"Jeez, where did I even go?"

"I have no idea. But you came back."

"This time."

"You have to help me."

"Do what?"

"Cooperate. Antwone's stuck in purgatory and you and I are the only ones who can release him into the universe."

"How? You got the secret code to open the doors to heaven?"

I lied. Getting Antwone into heaven was not part of my plan. My true intention was to keep him earthbound as long as possible, which I know makes me not a very good person.

"Go with me to St. Louis Cemetery tonight. We'll ask Marie Laveau to summon Antwone's spirit."

"I don't like the idea of going anywhere late at night anymore, especially not the cemetery."

"Don't worry. I have a knife," I said, "and I know how to use it."

That much was true. I had found an instructional video on the web called: "How to use a knife in a combative situation."

Following the instructions, I practiced flow drills in front of my mirrored closet slider every single night. There was more to it than I first thought. Algebra homework pushed aside, I devoted myself to studying Russian Speznatz knife fighting, South African techniques, and Filipino fighting styles. The chapter on prison knife fighting, which is one of the most scary and brutal things that anyone should ever hope to encounter, was extremely enlightening. I mastered the drills, and, in less than two weeks, I progressed all the way through level five, "Military quick kills, part two."

I don't care what anybody says, the internet is a fantastic educational tool. But Beano was still unconvinced.

"If the goal is to get Antwone into heaven, wouldn't it be smarter to go to a church instead of the grave of a dead voodoo queen?"

"Not according to The Betsy," I said.

"Oh hell, does she know what's going on?"

"Only hypothetically."

Unlike myself, Beano was, at heart, a good person, and even though he had reservations, he agreed to meet me at eleven that night at the corner of St. Louis and Chartres, across from the Napoleon House café.

One thing I knew for sure. You don't go to a voodoo queen's grave empty-handed. After school, I returned to the Voodoo Boutique where Miss Fleurette crafted an offering fit for a queen. She searched the shelves for the perfect gris gris bag and chose one made of leather, dyed red to evoke love and sex. She conjured a powerful concoction and mumbled incantations as she stuffed my gris gris with rare roots, herbs, botanicals, shells, sacred fetishes, and hand-pressed powders.

When she finished, she handed me the bag with one last caveat. "Always remember the contents are not as important as your own intent. What you believe is often truer than what is."

That night, I wrapped two small birch branches together with string in the shape of a cross, then snuck into the storeroom

and stole a bottle of Grand Marnier Cuvee Du Cent Cinquan-
tenaire Liqueur, one of the most expensive liqueurs in the bar.
I figured that it was bad form to show up at a classy voodoo
queen's grave with rock-gut whiskey. And when no one was
looking, I pilfered forty dollars from the cash box.

Around eleven, I plumped up pillows under the covers on my
bed to make an outline of a body in case my parents came into
my room. I wasn't really worried, because they hadn't checked
on me in the middle of the night since I was eight. Still, you
can't be too careful when engaging in clandestine activities.

Both Mary Ellen and Daddy were at the bar when I slipped
on Antwone's letterman jacket and snuck out of the apartment.
The Cock's Comb was in full swing. It was so loud and noisy in
the bar that I could have marched down the stairs with a brass
band and no one would have noticed.

Beano was waiting for me under a gas lamp when I turned
the corner to Chartres. Even from a distance, I could see how
scared he was. We hailed three cabs before we found the one
cabbie that would take us to the St. Louis Cemetery. Wizened
and prune-faced, he looked more like an elf than an old man
and he demanded ten dollars extra—combat pay, he called it—
to drive us to the cemetery. I agreed and we poured into the
backseat, which smelled like cigarettes and stale sweet potato
fries. As he turned down Basin Street, our elf/cabbie asked,
"You kids from out of town?"

"Certainly not," I said, slightly offended. "Why would you say
such a thing?"

"I figured only tourists would be stupid enough to go to St.
Louis at night. Because that cemetery is haunted by more than
just the dead."

"What do you mean?" Beano asked, getting more nervous by
the minute.

"I'm talking about those 'where ya at' boys from the Iberville
housing project who hunt down tourists and other idiots who
go to the St. Louis on their own. They rob those poor fools and
beat 'em so bad they wish they were dead already."

"First of all, they closed down the Iberville housing project after Katrina, so the only place that is possibly safer after the storm than it was before the storm is the St. Louis Cemetery," I said.

"Well, aren't you just full of information?" the elf/cabbie clucked.

"I practically live in a bar," I said. "People like to talk when they're drinking. And I like to listen."

"Well, missy, people talk when they're riding in cabs, and the cemetery is one dangerous place to be at night."

Beano sunk into the corner of the backseat, his face pressed against the window glass, as we zoomed through the neighborhood. The cabbie dropped us off at the front entrance of the Vieux Carre of the Dead and burned rubber as he sped away. There were no guards or hidden cameras. All that stood between the cemetery and us was a big iron lock on the filigreed front gate.

I went first. Using the scrolled ironwork as a foothold, I scrambled up the wall, avoided the jutting spikes at the top, leapt over to the other side, and landed on my feet. But Beano, who was the real athlete, didn't fare as well. He scaled the fence and paused at the top before heaving his body over to the other side. He fell with a heavy thud, ripped his jeans wide open, and skinned his knee. It was not pretty.

He lumbered to his feet, shivering as he got his bearings. I wasn't sure if his tremors were from nerves or the cool fall air. But either way, I convinced him to take Antwone's letterman jacket because I was toasty warm, feverish at the thought of seeing Antwone again.

We wove through the narrow passageways to the crypt of the voodoo priestess. Beano waited in the shadows as I approached her grave with my offerings. I knocked three times on the face of her tomb to wake her from the dead and sprinkled my offerings with the French liqueur.

"Oh, Marie Laveau, queen of voodoo, I lay this cross at your tomb in honor of your great faith and this gris gris in honor of the swamp magic in your veins. All this I bring to you in hopes that you will bring back my lost love, Antwone Despre. Beside me is my best friend and the willing host to Antwone's spirit. Thank you and amen."

"What now?" Beano asked.

"We wait," I said.

We stood, shifting uneasily back and forth for what seemed like an eternity.

"Feel anything?" I asked.

He shook his head. "We should have gone to church."

"Try to be a little more receptive," I said.

"Do you think the dead voodoo queen would mind if I had a little sip of her expensive French liqueur?" he asked.

"Go ahead. Maybe it'll help."

He did and then passed the bottle to me. I took a long drink. It tasted both sweet and bitter, liquid orange warm on my throat as it went down. Beano took three more hits before capping the bottle. We sat down together side by side on the cold concrete slab, waiting for the voodoo queen to do her magic.

Unsure and uneasy, I waited. After a bit, Beano nodded off, his head resting on my shoulder. A tremor surged through him that passed to me—I felt tingling in my fingertips—but he quickly stilled, his shallow breathing gradually deepening. I waited some more.

When a full hour had passed, I began to weep. If my mojo charms could not resurrect Antwone, maybe my tears would. But all my crying did was wake up Beano. He bolted upright, wide-eyed: "Is it over?"

"We never even began. Nothing's gonna happen tonight. We might as well head home."

We slipped out of the cemetery the same way we came in. There were no cabs to be had, but I wasn't frightened. I figured there weren't enough dangerous people left in the city to pose much of a threat. But I figured wrong. A few blocks from the

Cock's Comb, I caught a glimpse of a man coming out of a bar and walking toward us. As soon as I saw his Resident Evil baseball cap, I grabbed Beano's hand and ducked in an alleyway, hoping he didn't see me.

"Quick! Hide behind that dumpster," I hissed.

We dove behind the dumpster and I pulled the knife from the backpack.

"What the hell, Camille?" Beano asked.

I shushed him, but as we huddled together, I noticed a vial hanging around his neck. "What is that?" I whispered, gesturing to the small amulet.

"Holy water," he whispered back. "From the baptismal at St. Patrick's. I took it when the priest wasn't looking."

"Good lord, Beano. Everybody knows that holy water is a powerful antidote to voodoo."

"Hey, you have your magic and I have mine."

"Everything we did tonight—all the risks we took—was one big waste of time."

I was so angry that I yanked the amulet from Beano's neck and threw it on the ground. The tiny glass bottle shattered, and its contents drizzled onto the trash-littered alley.

"You in there, boo?" a voice called out from the entrance to the alleyway. "Don't try to hide from me. Come on out to Papa."

The sound of his work boots crunched on the cobblestones as he drew closer. I leapt out from behind the dumpster and landed about four feet from McGee. I crouched in a forward fighting stance, my weight resting evenly on the balls of my feet, my forward knee slightly bent, elbows close to my sides, my checking hand poised to attack, and my blade hand ready to strike.

"That's my knife, little girl," he said.

"It's mine now," I said, "and I know how to use it."

He laughed out loud at the very thought.

Our dance of combat began. I circled him like a tiger; his eyes never left me. I kept my distance, maneuvering until his back was facing the building at the end of the alley so that once I made my move, Beano and I would have a clear path to escape.

A rumble behind the dumpster distracted us both. A chill went right through me as McGee lunged forward and grabbed for the knife. But a karate-chop out of nowhere dislodged the knife from our collective grip and sent it skipping across the pavement. I turned and saw not Beano, but Antwone.

He punched McGee in the gut who doubled over in pain, then raised his fist for an uppercut. But before he could make contact, Antwone hit him again, this time hard in the face. His nose bleeding, possibly broken, McGee staggered backward. Antwone pushed his chest hard, knocking him into the dumpster. McGee's neck snapped back and he hit his head on the metal bin as he slid down to the pavement. I scrambled for the knife amid the debris, found it several feet away, and grabbed it up. We ran out of the alley, leaving McGee moaning.

We ran hard, crisscrossing through alleyways and streets until we reached the river. Finally, we stopped, breathless.

"Do you think you killed him?" I asked.

He shook his head. "Son-of-a-bitch's too mean to die, but I don't imagine he'll be bothering us anymore tonight."

I took Antwone's hand into my own. His knuckles were bruised and bleeding. There was an easiness between us; the rush of adrenaline from our near escape subsided, replaced by a soft intimacy. We walked along the banks of the Mississippi and talked for hours. I described what happened at Marie Laveau's tomb, how Beano's body convulsed in tremors.

"That was me," Antwone said. "But right as I entered, I was hit by something that sent me spinning back into the universe."

"I think it was the holy water Beano was wearing around his neck."

Antwone stopped, took a step away from me, and considered the implications. "If holy water repels me, then what am I? Some kind of devil?"

I assured him that he was not. In my mind, we had not witnessed a battle between good and evil, but a mix-up of magic. But the possibility of his belonging to the dark side depressed him beyond words.

"How do you know some shithead from the underworld doesn't own me outright?"

"I'll prove it to you."

Sometimes my own audacity surpasses that of my mother. We ran across Jackson Square and up the steps of the magnificent Cathedral-Basilica of Saint Louis. Its triple spire towered over us, as if in judgment. He hesitated at the door, but I drew him in.

"How else will we know?"

Together we crossed the threshold, and I gestured to the font. "Go ahead. Dip your hand into the holy water."

"What if you're wrong?" he asked, retreating.

I moved past him, plunged my cupped hands into the basin, scooped up a handful of blessed water, and raised it over his head. I opened my palms and let the water stream down his worried face. Nothing happened. He didn't vanish into thin air or dissolve into ashes or burst the cathedral into flames. "See, you are not a demon. You're an angel."

He laughed out loud. "One thing I know for sure. Whatever I am, I ain't no angel."

We slipped into a pew on the gospel side of the cathedral. He picked up a forgotten rosary and in the flickering light of votive candles, he talked about how angry he was at having died so young and left so much undone. As he opened up to me, he ran his fingers over the rosary by rote, which made me feel more like his confessor than his girlfriend.

"I'll never play college ball. Or go to law school. I wanted to make a real difference, ya' know? As dumbass as it sounds, I wanted to be that man the young boys look up to and the church ladies brag about."

"Your life mattered to the ones who matter most. It still matters."

He shrugged me off; he wasn't buying it. "All I feel is bad. I left everything so unfinished, especially stuff with M–."

There it was. We were back to M– again. I swallowed the bitterness I tasted every time he said her name.

"Ever think about why you keep appearing to me instead of her?"

"Maybe you were right. Maybe my coming back was to serve a higher purpose, and maybe that was to help you escape from the Cajun asshole in the alley. And if that's so, then maybe I'm finally done with here and can move on to wherever it is I'm supposed to go. Look, I don't understand any of this any better than you. Strange as it might seem, being dead does not make me an expert on—" he struggled to find the words. "On being dead."

He leaned over to nuzzle the top of my head. "One thing I do know. I've always liked your crazy-ass hair."

The stained glass windows to the east brightened, signaling the end of night and beginning of day. I couldn't explain the forces that brought us together, but I believed we were connected by a cosmic thread of longing and purpose held together across the borderlands between life and death.

He lifted my chin and kissed me softly on my forehead. I was not disappointed by his lack of passion. We were, after all, sitting in a church.

"It's getting light. And if this is my last night on Earth—"

"Don't say that," I interrupted.

But he continued: "If this is my last night on Earth, I'd like to see the river once more before daybreak."

He slipped his arm on my shoulder as we walked out of the sanctuary. We stepped out of the darkness into the pink gray of early morning, an hour before full dawn. But the contrast of dark to light was so great, I shaded my forehead and squinted. And in that split-second, I lost him once again. I turned to see my boyfriend gone and, in his place, my best friend.

"What happened?" Beano asked, running his fingers across

his knuckles, which I noticed were no longer scraped or bruised. When pressed, I gave him a G-rated version of the story. But he saw through me.

"Seems to me like you almost got us killed," Beano said, his voice cracking.

The sun was beginning to rise, and I knew I had to get home before my parents woke up. I suggested he grab a table at Café du Monde and wait for me. I promised that I'd join him shortly and explain everything.

He nodded and I sprinted across the empty square. I ran the four blocks to home, climbed the back stairs two at a time, and snuck back in with no one noticing. I quickly changed into my school uniform. I could hear Mary Ellen rummaging around in the kitchen, brewing the first pot of coffee. Before leaving, I took the knife from my backpack and put it back in its hiding place.

"Don't you want some breakfast?" she asked as I flew past her.

"I gotta catch the early bus," I told her as I scooted out of the apartment.

I knew I had to make Beano trust me again so that he would remain open to Antwone's spirit. I practiced my speech as I walked to the Café du Monde, but by the time I arrived at the bustling café, Beano was gone. He did not wait for me. He would not wait for me again. Not for a long time.

12.

Beano's in therapy," Gina told me on Saturday, grabbing another napkin to soak up the po'boy juice that dribbled down her chin. We were sitting at a picnic table outside our favorite midtown joint that overlooked the Bayou St. John. Like snowflakes, no two po'boys are exactly alike. Both Gina and I judged ours by the number of napkins we went through in the process of consuming them. The best ones were always a big, sloppy mess. My surf and turf, which combined tender roast beef and killer fried shrimp, ranked one napkin a bite. Gina's fried oyster po'boy was somewhat less perfect; she could get two, maybe three, bites per napkin. She rested her sandwich in the basket next to the sweet potato fries.

"He's going through a sexual identity crisis. He says he's been having strange heterosexual thoughts, like pornographic leftovers from somebody else's dreams."

I couldn't help but wonder if any of those thoughts were about me.

"Do you think the therapy is helping?" I asked, worried.

"Not really. Now he spends all his free time psychoanalyzing everybody else. Plus, he blames everything on the storm. He told me that I was sublimating my fear of death into a superficial desire to be popular."

"He has a point," I said. "I mean, you are running for student body president. Not really your thing pre-Katrina."

"So I've become more civic-minded," she said and then added quickly, "You are going to vote for me, right?"

"I promise. What does he say about me?"

"I don't think I should tell you."

"But you know you will," I replied. Gina could not keep a confidence for more than two minutes.

"Okay, fine. He says that you're holding onto the past. He also says that the reason you take unnecessary chances is to prove that you can be safe in an unsafe world."

"Are you going to finish that?" I asked, gesturing to her half-eaten sandwich. I had wolfed mine down, but ingesting Beano's psychobabble made me hungry all over again. She pushed the basket toward me and watched me finish it.

"What's going on with you, Camille? For real."

I lowered my gaze as I inhaled the last bite. I did not want her to see how deeply troubled I was. I worried that Beano might learn a defensive strategy in therapy to keep Antwone's spirit sequestered. But how could I tell my best friend that my other best friend was right? I was driven by a selfish desire to possess in death the love I never had in life. Even more terrifying was that Antwone's ghost was beginning to seem more real to me than the memory of him alive.

But I didn't share any of that with her. Instead, I washed down a handful of fries with an icy cold root beer dug down deep from the cooler and then took off for home. As I left, she called after me, "Someday soon, we gotta talk. Because I hardly know who you are anymore."

She was right about that. We had all been altered by the experience of Katrina. If not changed forever.

While I was having lunch with Gina, my parents closed the bar to meet with insurance brokers. I walked home, looking forward to some quality alone time with my cat. But instead of peace and quiet, I arrived at the scene of a crime.

In the courtyard, a police detective was interviewing Miz Cocktail, who was clearly shaken up by something or someone.

"What's going on? What happened? Where's my daddy?" I threw questions at her like wild pitches in the bottom of the ninth.

"Your momma and daddy are fine. They're on their way home now. But *we've* been robbed."

"As in the royal *we*?" I asked. Ever since my daddy left Miz Cocktail in charge after Katrina, she had assumed a kind of ownership of the Cock's Comb, so her use of "we" required clarification.

"So far, all that's missing is forty dollars from the cash box and a very expensive bottle of Grand Marnier."

I panicked. If the police dusted for prints in the storeroom, they most assuredly would find mine, which could be explained since I am a member of the household. But I was underage and had no business being in the liquor storeroom. My day suddenly had catastrophe written all over it.

I started for the apartment, but she called after me with a warning, "Camille, best not go up there now."

I ignored her and bounded up the stairs. All I could think was what if in all the hoopla they found my knife? The trouble I got into for buying sexy underwear would pale in comparison to the trouble awaiting me if my parents knew I had stolen a killing knife. I raced into the small living room and skidded to a stop. I couldn't believe it. Katrina herself could not have made a bigger mess. Our apartment was completely torn up by something more insidious than the storm. Drawers were emptied and dumped on the floor, their contents splattered with what looked like blood. The cushions on the couch were ripped open with the jagged edge of a knife. The walls were smeared with a yellowish brown. I almost threw up when I realized what it was: excrement. The thief had wiped his shit all over our apartment.

I stepped over broken dishes and stumbled toward my bedroom, but the long arm of the law stopped me cold. A cop appeared out of nowhere and grabbed my arm.

"Where do you think you're going, little lady?"

"My room," I said weakly.

I was worried sick. I asked him if anybody had seen a small

tabby. I knew that anybody who would rub poop on the wall would have no problem killing a cat.

"Don't worry, honey. Your daddy will buy you a new bed," Miz Cocktail said, walking in with the lead detective.

"Why? What's wrong with my bed?"

"Might not be a bad idea to let her have a look around her room. See if she notices anything missing," the detective told the cop.

I stepped over the threshold into an unrecognizable mess. I looked around. My laptop was where I left it, open on the desk, the screen shattered. As far as I could tell, nothing had been taken, but much had been destroyed. On the bed were piles of rags. I moved closer and recognized the slashed remnants of the only three nice dresses I owned—ripped from my closet, cut into pieces. As I moved closer still, I realized what was left of my dresses was soaked in urine.

He had pissed on my bed. And it smelled. Bad.

Just then, King Oliver jumped into the room from the open window. I scooped him up in my arms, nuzzled him gratefully, and put him down quickly before he could scratch me.

"Well, at least we have the perp's DNA," the detective said. "We'll run it through the system and see if we can find a match."

I didn't need a DNA sample to know who had done this to me. All the evidence I needed lay in an empty shoebox in the middle of the room pulled out from under the bed. Although it would never make the police report, the only thing missing from our house was my knife and I knew who had taken it.

I stalked him. I found out where he worked from an Alabama pipefitter, who had become a quitting-time regular at the Cock's Comb. He said McGee was a day laborer for a large demolition company tearing down a condemned warehouse on the wharves behind the French Market. Twice, I'd gone to the riverfront on my way home from school and caught a glimpse of the back of his sweaty shirt as he ripped out rotted boards and hauled them away into enormous trash bins. He didn't have the skill or training to become a drywaller, a carpenter, a plumber, or a steel worker. He was a bottom-feeder in the world of construction, doing the only thing he was qualified to do—destruction. Finishing what Katrina started, he added his own putrid stench to the mess she left behind.

I knew what kind of car he drove, a 1994 Grand Marquis, the color of black cherry ice. Its back fender was crushed, strapped to the chassis with black duct tape.

I knew what he ate for lunch; I saw the fast food wrappings in the back seat of his car. In a city known for its varied and wonderful cuisine, this guy who should have known better (he was no transplant from Ohio or Texas), what did he have every day for lunch? Not a po'boy or a deep-fried jalapeño stuffed with crab or a steaming bowl of jambalaya. Oh no, this native-born reprobate ate Taco Bell. But what would you expect from a guy who wiped his shit on my walls?

Midweek, I stopped by the construction site for a third time to do what I swore I would do on the first. I had hoped the police would identify him through the DNA sample, but he wasn't in the system. Evidently, he'd never been to prison, which was surprising to say the least. And I couldn't tell the authorities who he was because identifying him would mean implicating my own self in the business of the knife. I decided to handle McGee on my own. I became that girl Beano described—the one who took unnecessary chances. I could only imagine how Beano and his therapist would psychoanalyze what I was about to do.

I looked around; there was no sign of the crew. I supposed they were ripping up the inside of the warehouse, cleaning out rot and filth. But I noticed his car parked illegally on the other side of the street.

I crossed the street to investigate, still no sign of the construction workers. I reached his car and bent over to peer through the side window. Dust and grime clouded the glass; inside was a blurred mess of fast food wrappers. I could see a stained pillowcase and a raggedy quilt shoved into the corner. It looked like he lived in his car.

I wondered if the knife he stole back from me was somewhere inside. McGee was careless; that much I knew. I doubted that he even bothered to lock up his car. Why would he? His Marquis was no longer grand. It was hardly a target for thieves. I jiggled the door handle. It was locked.

"Wanna go for a ride, boo?" a voice asked behind me. His Cajun term of endearment sent shivers down my spine.

I whipped around to see him towering over me. I had forgotten how tall he was. His shoulders seemed even broader; he had bulked up since I last saw him. Evidently hauling trash was as good as lifting weights at the gym. He was so close I could smell the stench of stale beer on his breath.

"What you doing here? You got some kinda schoolgirl crush on me?"

"I know you broke into our apartment."

"You tell the police that?"

"No."

"I was right. You do have a crush on me."

"How'd you know the place'd be empty?"

"Your daddy told the regulars they were opening the bar late, and one of them told me."

I imagined it was the loose-lipped pipefitter from Alabama who told me about McGee.

"I ain't gonna lie. I'd hoped to find you home alone. I had big plans for us."

"Don't you ever come near me or my family again. That's all I came to say."

"Or what?"

"Or you'll be sorry."

He grabbed my arm and held me firm. "You remind me of someone, boo. Someone from a long time ago. She was feisty, too. But not for long. They never fight for too very long," he said, breathing down my neck.

He pushed me toward the car door. I panicked. If he came at me, how would I fight him off?

"What you up to, brother? That girl's a little young, even for you," yelled one of the hardhats as he exited the site with a couple others from the crew.

"I caught her trying to break into my car," he yelled back.

"Want me to call the cops?" he hollered.

"No need," McGee let me go and whispered in my ear. "See you around, cher. You can count on it."

And with that, he slipped into the front seat, slammed the door, and revved up the engine. He pulled the Grand Marquis away from the curb and then gunned it, burning rubber in its wake. I did not relax until his black cherry sedan completely faded from view.

With startling clarity, I realized just how right the elf/cabbie who had driven Beano and me to the St. Louis Cemetery had been. The most dangerous and frightening souls in New Orleans were not among the dead; they were among the living. And this one had left his mark on me.

The next morning, I took the bus to the Salon Batiste, which had recently re-opened with the return of its owner. As I waited my turn in her chair, an elderly lady with silver braids twisted into bantu knots said, "Everybody I've talked to who's come back to New Orleans can point to that one thing that turned them back around. What called you home, honey?"

Aisha's older sister, who owned a big old house near the bird preserve on Sanibel Island, had urged her to stay, but gradually a deep longing took hold, something stronger than even fear.

"It was all about the gumbo. I mean I could get okra in Florida. Tomatoes, too. And seafood was plentiful. But I had to drive thirty-six miles to find me some Andouille sausage. And nobody seemed to think that was a problem," Aisha said, smiling and turning her attention to me. "But the real reason I came back is Camille. Look at this child's hair."

"She needs your skills," the lady said as she teetered out of the salon on her hand-carved cane like the Queen of England.

Aisha examined by head, running her fingers through my tangles. I closed my eyes, luxuriating in the feeling of her silky fingers on my scalp. "Good lord, how long has it been since somebody laid a hand on your head?"

Aisha's voice was so sweet and melodic that even when she chided you, it sounded like love.

"I've been waiting for you to get back, 'cause I want to do something different with my hair. I want to wear it wild and crazy."

"How wild?" she asked.

"Well, not wild like it is now. Not out-of-control wild. But wild in a beautiful way."

"We can relax the curls, but you'll have to stay out of the water."

"I don't want to stay away from the water. I want to immerse myself in it."

She spun the chair around and fixed her gaze on me. "What did you go and do while I was gone?"

She told me to follow her, and, on our way out the back exit, Aisha stopped at the storeroom and pulled out a tin box marked For Emergencies Only. Inside was a half-opened package of herbal cigarettes called Honeyrose Clove. She pulled out one, along with a box of matches, and then closed the box, returning it to the top shelf for safekeeping, presumably until the next crisis.

Standing outside in the alley, she lit the cigarette and took a long drag; smoke curled from her lips. After a long but comfortable silence, she finally spoke.

"Who did you lose in the storm?" she asked matter-of-factly.

You could have pushed me over with a feather. "How did you know?" I asked.

"I could smell death in the room all tangled up with love."

"His name is Antwone Despre. He lived next door to me."

I gave her an abbreviated account of what I knew of his death and how I had felt his presence since. I left out a few important details, like Beano's involuntary involvement, because when you're doing a thumbnail sketch of a ghost visitation, saying something like, "My dead boyfriend comes to me in the body of my best friend, a gay football player," just makes you sound crazy. But as it turns out, those details interested her less. She went straight to the funeral; that's what she wanted to know about.

"There hasn't been one yet. His body was never found, and his grandmother refuses to have a service without a body," I explained.

Aisha was upset. "Well, that's just wrong. When a spirit is looking for release, you have to help it along."

"But what if he's not ready to go? What if he's stuck here for a reason?"

"Child, you must relinquish your earthly hold on him. The next time he makes his presence known to you, you must give him permission to leave the living behind. Assure him that he will live forever in the stories of the lives he has touched."

I lied and said that's exactly what I'd been trying to do when I braved my way to the grave of Marie Laveau at midnight, slightly altering some of the facts to put my motivations in a better light. Aisha shook her head, tallying up my mistakes one by one.

"First of all, you went to the wrong grave. Marie Laveau is not buried in the Glapion family crypt. That tomb holds the bones of her daughter, the other Marie Laveau. The mother, the real and most powerful voodoo queen, is buried in St. Louis Cemetery No. 2 in the Faubourg Tremé. And there's no reason to wait until nightfall; voodoo is just as powerful in the light of day. If you go back, and I'm not saying you should, but if you go again, don't insult the woman with chicken feed or chicken feet. You give her the two things she can't get in heaven: money and booze."

I asked her if she would draw me a map to her grave because the last thing I wanted to do was get it wrong twice.

She nodded and as she drew me a map of the cemetery, she told me more about the legendary voodoo queen of New Orleans, how she never abandoned her Catholic roots but incorporated Christian ritual with her mother's African traditional beliefs. A free person of color and part Choctaw, Marie Laveau was widely praised as a living saint for her humanitarian gestures. She healed the sick and ministered to the poor and imprisoned. She was also greatly feared; stories circulated about what had happened to those who had offended her. Rich and poor, Black and white—all sought the aid of her dark powers to summon lovers, gain fame and fortune, or to exact revenge.

"What you may not know, and many have forgotten, is that the root of her enduring legend began with the sanctity of the hair. Before she was a voodoo queen, she was the best hairdresser in the Quarter," Aisha said, taking pride in the voodoo queen's connection to her own noble profession.

She stubbed out her cigarette with the toe of her high-heeled wedged boots, and we went back inside to do something with my hair. She combed it, trimmed it, and washed it so clean my scalp tingled. It took her just under two hours to braid the front into zigzag cornrows that stopped just past my ears. The rest flowed in rivers of frizz, like a beehive at the back of my head. When I looked in the mirror, I liked what I saw.

My new hair and I walked through the Quarter, mulling over what Aisha had said. A light autumn rain had begun to fall, so the streets were emptier than usual; people ducked into bars and shops. But not me. I welcomed the rain. The tiny droplets falling on my face felt like tears. It had been five weeks since Antwone's last visitation, and I missed him so bad it hurt. I came home and hid myself away in my room. Much later, under the light of a new moon, I fashioned three crosses out of birch and waited for the dawn.

I hardly slept at all.

Early the next morning, I slipped into the bar on my way out, took most of the coins from the tip jar, grabbed a red plastic go-cup, poured two healthy shots of bourbon into my thermos, packed it all up into my St. Bede's backpack, and stepped out into the day. I caught the first morning bus to the Faubourg Tremé and got off near the oldest Creole cemetery in New Orleans. Covering three city blocks, it was not too far from Congo Square where the original voodoo rites had been staged by Marie Laveau herself. As I walked through the narrow, winding passageways, I could see lingering water lines, reminders of the flood. Using Aisha's hand-drawn map as a guide, I found the voodoo queen's crypt marked with Xs scratched in groups of three.

Shaking with excitement, I poured the bourbon into the go-cup, placed it on the ground, and arranged the three handmade crosses painted in Mardi Gras colors around it. I knocked three times on the crypt, threw the coins into the bourbon, closed my eyes, and began:

"Oh, great Queen, I come to you because you are the priestess of voodoo magic. You have helped so many others in matters of the heart, both when you lived and now that you have gone. I call on your authority to help me reach beyond to one who has passed—the one I love—the one I wish to see again."

"You yourself have the power to call him back. You've proven that twice. Why come to me?"

I opened my eyes to see who had spoken. Like mist rising from the swamp, a ground fog crept across my handmade altar in front of the crypt. Trembling, I answered the woman I could not see, using what I had learned from Aisha about the voodoo queen's life to bolster my own plea.

"I come to you because you know what it means to love someone you cannot fully possess. You lived for thirty years with a Christopher Glapion. You bore him fifteen children. All the while ministering to those in need. Healing the wounded. Practicing your brand of Catholic voodoo religion. You walked through the streets of New Orleans as if you owned them; respect followed you everywhere. But you were not allowed to marry the father of your children because he was white and you were Black. And in that way, something was taken away from you that should have been rightfully yours. Something has been taken from me, too."

Suddenly, the mist swirled and swept over my body, enveloping the tomb. And on the face of the tomb, I saw another face, that of a woman. She was beautiful, flawless, a timeless beauty etched in stone. Her lips did not move when she spoke, but I could hear her words inside my head, playing like the melody of a familiar song.

"The longer you hold onto him, the harder it will be. Let him go and be done with it."

I thought about fudging the truth as I had done with Aisha and with The Betsy because I was getting pretty good at it. But I figured a dead voodoo queen would see through my intent to the depths of my soul.

"I will gladly suffer the consequences of being with him again, however hard it may be."

Her voice softened with empathy. "You alone can set him free so that he can move on from this world to the next. One word from you. A little assurance. Something that shows him you can look out after your own sweet self and be kind to the ones he loved and left behind—that's all it would take."

"I want to do what's right, but not if it means I can't ever be with him again."

Soft words whispered at the back of my neck. "If I agree to help you, what will you give me in return?"

"Anything you ask."

"Anything?" she repeated.

"Yes."

"Will you swear on your immortal soul that if I bring him back, in return you will let him go?"

"How much time will we have together? A year? A month? One long night?"

I was surprised by my brazenness. So was she.

"You dare to haggle with Marie Laveau like she was some common shopkeeper, trading slabs of beef for sugar?"

"I meant no disrespect. I humble myself before you."

Evidently, my apology appeased her because she continued: "I will bring him back to you on Twelfth Night and he will stay as the gods allow through the whole of Mardi Gras. But when the revelers go home and the last of the beads are swept off the street, you must give him up for Lent."

I took a deep breath and swore an oath.

Her face disappeared from the tomb and was sucked into the mist, which swirled off the rock and slammed into me with a power so intense that it knocked me to my knees. I lay on the cold, hard ground, trying to make some sense of what I had just seen or imagined.

As the soft morning light danced across the whitewashed crypts, I left the bourbon and crosses at the tomb of the dead queen and took a tentative step away from the supernatural and back into the real world.

It had begun to rain; a soft whisper of water covered the city. I didn't have to wait long for a bus and gratefully slid into a seat at the back. I leaned my head against the window, and, with eyes half-closed, watched as the early morning Sunday broke on streets, damp and glistening. I had drifted into a peaceful slumber, light as the rain that fell, when I felt the piercing intrusion of something cold and dark. The presence of evil. I opened my eyes, but the bus was empty. I was all alone with nothing but the memory of my sworn oath to a dead voodoo queen and the knowledge I would have to wait for an entire month to see if it would come true.

13.

December dragged on forever. Midway through, Gina lost the election for student body president by a landslide. Our principal, Sister Mary Benedict, announced the winner in an all-school assembly late Friday afternoon in an effort to avoid emotional meltdowns. It did not work. Mind you, we all were a little unhinged in the months following the storm, but that afternoon Gina blew the roof off crazy.

As the newly installed student body president, William Renfro, took the podium with Sister Mary Benedict, Gina tore through the crowd screaming that the nuns had rigged the election. Even I questioned her logic. Over the years, the nuns had been accused of many things at St. Bede's, but election fraud was not among them.

Gina ran to the podium, grabbed the mic from a shell-shocked William Renfro, and began a non-stop tirade on why the nuns had sabotaged her campaign.

"I have been denied public office because I dyed my hair purple when I was a freshman," Gina screamed, "and because I roll up the waistband on my skirt to make it shorter so that sometimes you can see my underwear. And, yes, I wear a thong."

Students reacted—some looked confused, others were embarrassed. But the ones who counted, like M— and her girls, the ones who decided the social fate of the rest of us, watched, fascinated and clearly collecting fodder for the future. Beano and I exchanged a look; our best friend was single-handedly turning herself—and, by association, us—into social pariahs.

"She needs to keep her panties out of politics," Beano whispered to me.

"If she goes on much longer, we're toast. I'll grab the diva and you get the car," I answered.

Like a salmon swimming upstream, I charged into the crowd, reached the front, and dragged Gina away from the scene of her social crime and into the parking lot. We poured into Beano's red Hyundai, engine revving.

And we got the hell out of town.

Gina sobbed for ten miles; she could not be consoled. The way she cried was downright irritating, like the high-pitched whir of a smoke detector alarm going off. Finally, Beano slammed on the brakes.

"I need a beer."

"And I could use some sausage," I said.

Both were easily obtainable, if you didn't mind driving across Lake Pontchartrain in Friday afternoon traffic. On the other side of the twenty-three-mile bridge was a rickety old gas station that once was used for hog butchering and was now home to possibly the best Boudin sausage west of New Iberia. The owner of the gas station was a Greek man who was married to a Cajun woman with a hundred-year-old recipe for sausage. I don't know if it was because he was European or because he was an anarchist, but the old man could not be bothered with technicalities like liquor laws. He figured if you were smart enough to find his place, tall enough to reach the bar, sober enough to order it, and rich enough to pay for it, who was he to refuse you a cold draft beer? For the most part, the cops left him alone, because if they shut him down, they would have to make the two-hour-plus drive to New Iberia to get links half as good.

Beano and Gina ordered the Boudin Blanc, which contained fatty sausage without the blood. I preferred the Boudin Rouge. Some folks are put off by the blood component, but I found the flavor—hearty, dense, complex, and earthy—to be satisfying on a deeper level. As far as I was concerned, without the blood it wasn't Boudin.

There, over a plate of homemade link sausage and a cold draft beer, Gina let go of her political aspirations. And when she went home that night, she died her hair magenta.

It was good to have our Gina back.

I called the Cock's Comb from the mansion in the Garden District and told Mary Ellen I was spending the night. She was not surprised; she knew how much I hated our apartment. She assumed it was because it was too small for the three of us. She was wrong. I was used to close quarters; the proximity of my parents' bedroom to mine was not what drove me away. It was the smell in my own room. After the break-in, Mary Ellen and I scrubbed the walls and floors with Clorox bleach. We repainted my bedroom. We threw out the mattress and the linens and replaced them with fresh new bedding. Even still, late at night, the stench of urine returned, wafting up through the floorboards, keeping me awake.

"I've made a decision," Gina announced, blow-drying her purplish red locks. "I know just how to undo my bad and get us reinstated into the social hierarchy."

It's not like we wanted to be one of the popular kids. We just wanted to sit in the cafeteria and eat our lunch without incident.

"What are you going to do? And please tell me it does not involve running for anything," I asked, hopefully.

"Don't worry. I'm through with politics. I'm going to throw a kick-ass Twelfth Night party to start the season. And I'm going to invite the whole school. Okay, maybe not William Renfro or M— and her mean girls. But everybody else."

You might suppose that after her election speech debacle, no one at St. Bede's would come to a party given by Gina, but you would suppose wrong. Because in New Orleans, even the most horrific of social crimes could be erased in a nanosecond with an all-night party in a Garden District mansion at the home of The Betsy.

What Gina did not know was that in her attempt to reinstate us socially, she had unknowingly given me back the birthday party I had dreamed about, where Antwone and I would finally get together, as promised by the dead voodoo queen. I was the happiest girl in all of New Orleans.

I spent the rest of December channeling my energy into putting together my costume for Gina's party. I was even able to convince Beano that Antwone's spirit had moved on, so we became close again. He even agreed to be my personal shopper, to transform me into something that would attract "a real boyfriend." Beano, as both a gay man and a member of the football team, was in a unique position to do just that. I was grateful for his help, because he was also a master creator of spectacularly sexy costumes.

We landed on the idea of a sexy pirate's wench, but as I was searching through the back room of a thrift shop on Canal Street for a starched petticoat, I discovered a pair of sheer gossamer wings, almost as long as I was tall.

I showed the wings to Beano and Lewis, who had become annoyingly glued to his side of late. His boyfriend did not share my enthusiasm.

"Pirate wenches are bad girls. They don't sprout angel wings," Lewis said, turning up his nose at my new find.

"Well, obviously, the wings change our whole concept," I said. "I don't know why, but these wings speak to me."

"That's because they are beyond fabulous," Beano agreed. "I can picture the whole thing. We'll borrow one of The Betsy's old ball gowns. I seem to remember a gold velvet brocaded number with Juliet sleeves that would be perfect. With the right makeup and an ultra-super push-up bra, you could do Drew Barrymore from *Ever After*."

"Too much baggage. I could never pull it off. Besides, I'd rather be a butterfly than a princess."

"Which would require a unitard. Seriously, Camille, do you want to expose your muffin-top for all the world to see?"

"No worries. The muffin-top has miraculously disappeared."

"Oh my god, you are so right," Beano exclaimed as I modeled a sleek black unitard with a gold lame bodice and diamond cutouts in the back.

While others wrapped gifts for Christmas, I sewed beads onto the wings in intricate and dramatic patterns that Beano stenciled for me to follow. Mary Ellen viewed my handiwork with judgmental sighs, especially when I asked if I could have money instead of a Christmas present so I could buy yet more beads and baubles. But Donald delighted in my new obsession. He said that for a hundred years, some decked-out Darveau had either ridden on a Mardi Gras float or fallen off one. He was proud of me for following the beat of my own Mardi Gras drum.

And even after the gifts were unwrapped and the Christmas goose demolished, the work continued. No one in New Orleans that year took costuming more seriously than I, not even the Mardi Gras Indians.

But unlike the Mardi Gras Indians, who often sewed on the last bead just as the first chant of "Hey Pocky Way" began, I finished my wings the morning of the party, which wouldn't start until midnight. As soon as I tied the last knot, I packed a bag, threw on Antwone's letterman jacket, and cabbed it to Gina's with my winged creations in tow to help decorate the house for the party.

I arrived to a mess of purple, green, and gold chaos. Boxes of beads carried down from the attic crowded the dining room. The Betsy bragged that if she laid out her strands of Mardi Gras beads collected over the years, bead to bead, they would make a party chain long enough to wrap around the circumference of the earth at least twice.

Gina and I worked for hours, filling glass bowl centerpieces with baubles, draping beads on chandeliers, placing mounds of them on the mantelpiece. We stripped the Christmas tree of its ornaments and layered it with so many strands of colorful beads that the green tips of the branches were barely visible.

All that and we barely made a dent in the boxes. The Betsy supervised from behind the pages of *The Times Picayune*. One thing about The Betsy—I have never seen her do any real work. She liked to say her calling was to inspire others.

"Blasphemy!" The Betsy exclaimed, looking up from the paper. "Our city leaders have lost their minds."

Her outburst startled me and I almost fell off the stepladder where Gina and I were rigging a harlequin head to a Schonbek crystal chandelier.

"It's just not right," The Betsy went on. "They want to scale back Mardi Gras this year, if not cancel it altogether."

"Can they do that?" I asked, my throat tightening.

"They sure as hell better not try," The Betsy said, throwing the paper into the trashcan. "Or else they'll hear plenty from me. We're not like those idiots in Washington D.C. who act like any day now the government's gonna come up with a cure for death. Down here we know that you don't live forever and that the only defense against the Grim Reaper is a life well lived. And if that means sometimes drinking too much champagne or eating a little too much sugar or falling in love with the wrong man, well, so be it. Cancel Mardi Gras, my ass. Our city leaders had best recommit to the voodoo Catholic soul of this city and come to the damn party."

Exhausted by her tirade, The Betsy retired to her boudoir for a little nap.

It was close to ten-thirty when I stepped out of the shower, dripping wet. As I grabbed a towel, my cell rang. It was Beano; he was all upset because Lewis was sick as a dog. Having discovered that he loved being part of a couple, Beano said he didn't feel like coming without his better half.

My senses gave way. I couldn't see; I couldn't hear. It was like drowning in the void of my increasingly loud heartbeat. I couldn't believe it. All my plans, my dreams, my reason for living these past six weeks gone.

"Camille, are you still there?" Beano asked.

I turned to Gina: "Beano says he's not coming because Lewis is sick."

Gina paused from shadowing her Cleopatra eyes, put down her brush, rose from her vanity table, and grabbed my cell from me.

"If you miss my Twelfth Night party because your boyfriend is a little under the weather, then you are no longer a citizen of this city. Or my friend. Stop your whining, get your ass over here, and help me with my hair."

Sometimes, Gina sounded just like her mother. And for that, I was forever grateful.

14.

Beano showed up half an hour later in a costume that was magnificent even by his impossible standards. Dressed as a prince from the court of Marie Antoinette, he wore baby blue embroidered breeches, a gold waistcoat with six-inch cuffs enriched with fake diamonds, and real leather gloves.

A little before midnight, the three of us, medieval punk princess Gina, a gloved and masked Beano, and butterfly-me descended the winding staircase into a Twelfth Night wonderland. The entire downstairs was lit with hundreds of candles whose soft glow caught the shimmer of the Mardi beads piled high in silver bowls. Off the living room, the adjoining patio had been converted to a dance floor lined with heat lamps. A local DJ was cuing up the playlist Gina had painstakingly made.

We only had a moment to take it all in before the doorbell rang and guests began to arrive in droves—all costumed, mostly masked. I was one of the few unmasked revelers, but everyone loved my costume. Their compliments meant nothing to me. The only person whose opinion mattered had not yet appeared. I stayed glued to Beano's side, waiting for Antwone's arrival.

But he didn't show. Not at twelve with the first wave of guests. Not by twelve-thirty as revelers began spiking their wassail punch with hidden flasks of stolen booze. Not by one when a two-hundred-pound lineman ran into me and sloshed his drink onto my gold unitard, staining the bodice cranberry red. Not by one-thirty when the dance floor was packed with sweating bodies. Not by two when my wings began to fold, knocking me about my head. And not by two-thirty, when M— and her girls made a grand entrance.

"Did you invite her?" I hissed at Gina.

"Of course not," she hissed back.

M— was dressed in a gold brocade gown with sheer gossamer wings almost identical to my own. She swept into the room to an audible gasp from the crowd. We were two winged creatures—she and I. Only she looked like a for real *Ever After* princess. I suddenly felt like a three-year-old at a dance recital about to perform "Flight of the Bumblebee."

I expected her to pause dramatically and take in in the crowd's adoration, but instead she made a beeline for me, insisting that we needed to talk. We stepped out onto the balcony, and I closed the door behind us. She pulled a silver flask from the folds of her heavy gown.

"Wanna shot?" M— said, all saccharin sweet.

I took a sip, expecting vodka mixed with Diet Coke because that's what popular girls drink. Taken aback, I gagged.

"No offense, but that's just about the worst thing I ever tasted."

"I'm not surprised you don't care for it. Peppermint schnapps is an acquired taste."

I ignored her air of superiority as she told me that over Christmas break she had gone to Baton Rouge to visit Bama, who had moved in with her other sister shortly after Auntie Shay's funeral.

"How is she?" I asked, weighted down with equal parts beads and guilt. I had been so obsessed with my Mardi Gras wings that I hadn't even called Bama, much less arranged to go see her.

"I think she's beginning to get used to the idea that he's gone. I still can't shake the feeling that he's just a heartbeat away, but I know your daddy was telling the truth. We lost him in the storm."

"Well, thanks for telling me about Bama," I said, attempting to leave both the cold and the conversation.

"There's something more. When I talked to Bama, she said that your mother had salvaged some stuff from the storm, Antwone's things among them. She said it was okay for me to go through the boxes and pick something out. She said it pleased her that I wanted something to remember him by."

"Like what?" I asked.

"Well, he had a beautiful old watch. He told people it had belonged to his grandfather, but I was with him when he bought it in a pawnshop on Canal. And it was expensive. He had wonderful taste in jewelry."

"Yes, he did," I said, sliding the chain of my necklace to the back of my neck so that the fleur-de-lis was out of sight. "But the watch wasn't among the things we found."

"Okay, then. I'd like to have his letterman jacket."

"I'll ask my mother, but I don't recall finding it."

"You're lying. And I have proof. I want that jacket, Camille, and you're gonna give it to me."

"We'll see about that."

I huffed back into the party just in time to witness the grand entrance of two huge king cakes or the *Galette des Rois*, sprinkled in sugar-dyed Mardi Gras colors. The guests were surprised. Generally, the presentation of the king cake was near the end of the party and we had hours to go before dawn.

Gina stepped up on an antique coffee table, artfully avoiding a collection of ceramic pugs.

"I know it's a little early, but tonight we're going to start a new tradition. As you can see there are two cakes. One for the guys and one for the girls. And whoever gets the slices containing the Carnival baby will be declared the queen and king of St. Bede's Twelfth Night.

"And here's the really good part. As king and queen, the royal couple can command anyone at the party to do anything, just as long as *it is something that they would not normally do*."

Everyone crowded the table to get their slice of cake. Nothing is more seductive than having unlimited power over your classmates. Halfway through the gents' cake, Beano pulled the plastic baby from between his teeth and held it up for the crowd to see. All the straight men in the room shuddered to think what an openly gay man, flying solo without his boyfriend, might ask them to do. The possibilities were staggering.

There were only two pieces of cake left and still no queen. "Who doesn't have cake?" Gina asked the girls.

"Me," I answered, coming forward and taking the next to last slice.

"And M–!" one of her girls shouted as the princess herself returned from the balcony.

I looked at the piece of cake I held and the piece remaining. I thought I noticed what might be a baby bump on the last slice of cake—the one destined for M–. She might look like a princess, but I'll be damned if I was going to let her be queen.

"Here, take this one," I said, offering M– the plate with the piece of cake I chose first and taking the last slice for myself.

I poked my fork into the baby bump, which as it turned out was almond frangipane filling. I kept stabbing, drilling for the baby, and decimating the puff pastry in the process.

"Good lord, Camille, it's not a race," Beano whispered, embarrassed by my surge of competitiveness.

In the end, it didn't matter.

All eyes turned from me to M–. As soon as she put the first fork into the pastry, she stabbed plastic. The baby rolled onto her plate.

"We have our king and queen of the St. Bede's Ball," Gina announced as she placed jeweled crowns on the heads of my best friend and my archenemy.

My heart sank.

It started out innocently enough. Beano began by asking the president of the glee club to faux strip to The Pussycat Dolls. M– then commanded an offensive lineman to sing "I Feel like a Natural Woman" in schoolgirl falsetto. Someone had to burp his name. Somebody else had to take a shot of ketchup and snort like a pig, which was all fine and good, but when crowd enthusiasm began to wane, Beano regained center stage by making the homophobic Jason Jones lick some poor boy's eyeball. Not to be outdone, M– coated a banana with peanut butter and then commanded Agnes, the shyest girl in the school—one of the invisibles—to suck it off. If M–'s goal was to embarrass her, it backfired. Agnes went after that banana like a five-hundred-dollar whore in the back seat of a limo. Within five minutes, half the graduating class had added her contact info to their phones. And not just the boys. Girls, too, because they figured anybody who could lick peanut butter off a banana without damaging the fruit was somebody worth knowing.

And so, it continued. There were fake orgasms ordered up, bunny face drawings with lipstick, death scenes performed. One of the laziest boys in the senior class had to call his folks and ask if it was okay if he spent the entire next day doing chores. That I thought was funny.

But Beano crossed the line when he demanded that Gina, without using her hands, put a piece of gum into the mouth of the guy who upstaged her by winning the student body presidency.

"Okay, we are done with this game!" Gina shouted to protests from the guests who felt it was only fair that she get her just desserts since it was her dessert that started the whole mess.

"How about letting each of us have one more turn? Then we call it a night," M– suggested. Gina could not say no without looking like a bad sport, so she agreed.

M– pointed straight at me. "I command Camille to give me Antwone's letterman jacket."

"I already told you I don't have it."

A hush fell over the room. Gina knew I had the jacket; it was upstairs lying on the chaise in her bedroom. But she covered for me anyway.

"If Camille had the jacket, she'd give it to you. Come up with something else," Gina said.

"Oh, she has it all right. My girl Ebony saw her wearing it in the Quarter."

I was surrounded by whispers and accusations; the court of public opinion was not on my side. Gina squeezed my hand.

"I'm sorry, Camille."

"It's not your fault." But I said it in a way that made it clear that I did believe it was her fault. For starting this stupid game in the first place.

"Bring it to school Monday morning," M— said in a downright threatening tone. A chill ran down my spine.

"My turn," the king of St. Bede's Twelfth Night said, stepping forward.

"Well, do it already, so we can get back to the dance floor," Gina said. "What is your last command?"

"I want a kiss. From my queen."

"What you been smoking? 'Cause you must be high." M— was as surprised as the rest of us. Everyone waited for what would come next, none with more interest than me.

Our king unmasked and revealed the man underneath. My best friend had disappeared and, in his place, stood my dead boyfriend, brought back as promised by voodoo magic. I watched helplessly as Antwone leaned in to kiss M—, who followed his gaze with eyes wide open. The whole damn school stood as silent witness. It unfolded like a stunning movie screen kind of kiss, beginning with the tender brushing of lips. Once. Twice. And once more before she finally closed her eyes and relaxed her lips, inviting his tongue to enter her mouth. As he kissed her deeply, he moved his hand to the small of her back and pressed her body into his. She did not resist; she welcomed him. I didn't realize that I had begun to cry until I tasted the salt of my own tears as they ran down my cheeks to my lips.

When he finally released her, she stepped back, unsteady on her feet. He took her hand so she could get her balance. And when she regained her footing, she smiled and started to pull back, but he turned her hand over in his and brought it to his lips, kissing the inside of her wrist, the place where scent and heartbeat meet.

She forced a laugh. "I'll give you this. For a gay guy, you sure know how to kiss a woman."

In my heart, I knew that he had hoped that she would see him the way I did, that she would sense his presence. But she clearly did not. On his face was profound disappointment.

Gina threw open the French doors to the patio where loud hip-hop music and an empty dance floor beckoned. M— started out with the others, but Antwone pulled her back and whispered something in her ear. She jerked back like she'd been slapped and then left in one big hurry, eager to create distance between herself and him. Once outside, the crowd literally parted for her so she could join her girls, who had grabbed a prime piece of real estate on the dance floor. From inside, Antwone watched M— command attention with her pop and lock—seductive moves that were once meant just for him.

He ran out of the room. I followed close on his heels, but my wings got caught on the entry hall doorframe, and hundreds of beads scattered across the floor, spilling out like a jarful of marbles.

Antwone slammed out of the house with a heart full of hurt. I chased him down the steps, yelling for him to stop, but he took off running down the street. I worried that if Antwone disappeared into New Orleans and Beano returned in unfamiliar surroundings, my best friend might freak out and get into real trouble. Out of breath and panting, I yelled as he reached the intersection, "Haven't you got our friend into enough trouble for one night?"

He stopped and turned back around. Lit by the soft light of the one working streetlight on the whole block, his face was lined with a pain so raw it could make you cry. He walked back in my direction and when he reached me, he took my hand.

"I was so sure M— would know who I was. The same way you do."

"Well, now we know."

If only Antwone could see her with the same clarity that I saw him. He would know who she was. Cold. Heartless. Shallow. Hand in hand, we walked back to Gina's mansion and parked ourselves on an iron bench under a hundred-year-old oak in the front yard.

"I think I really messed up," he said.

"How?"

"I told her the truth, but she didn't take it too well."

Now I was really worried. Since dying, Antwone was as fervent about truth-telling as a born-again Christian is about salvation. He clung to veracity like it was deliverance.

"Exactly what did you say?"

"I told her that I loved her and that she was right about me being a player. My problem was that I thought I could have it both ways."

"Oh my god."

"What?"

"Don't you see? You outed Beano as a bisexual, which is problematic on so many levels."

He paused, measuring the effect his words would have coming out of what appeared to be Beano's mouth.

"Damn, tell him I'm sorry, okay?"

"I'm not going to tell him anything. It's all fine and well for you to be so honest now that you've passed to the other side, but here in New Orleans, the truth is not without consequence."

"You are preaching to the choir, baby girl."

"About what?"

"Truth. And consequences. I screwed up, Camille, and it took me dying to figure it out."

As mad as I was at him for not loving me the way he did her, I couldn't stand seeing him so upset.

"Don't be so hard on yourself. The Betsy says that men have to grow into good, that most of them aren't worth shit until they turn thirty-two."

He dropped his head into his hands. "I'll always be eighteen. You ever think about that? With no chance to grow into good."

Antwone recounted his history with M— and every misstep he took. He admitted that her suspicions about his being unfaithful were not completely unfounded.

"Thing is, I had convinced myself that what I was doing wasn't wrong. 'Cause I didn't ask girls to leave panties in my locker. Or to call me in the middle of the night for phone sex. But after a while I began to believe that if I didn't ask for it and they were offering it up, I must somehow deserve it. I figured that I would grow into faithful, you know, when I got older."

"So, M— was right? You cheated on her?"

"Not technically. I didn't *sleep* with any of those girls."

"Well, what did you do?"

"Oh, you know, this and that."

I didn't know what to say or how to comfort him, when my own heart was breaking. The worst thing about his confession was that it made me feel like he had cheated on me, too. The sky began to turn a misty rose and as night gave way to day, he noticed the necklace dangling from my neck for the first time.

"You found it," he said as he reached over to touch the filigreed fleur-de-lis charm.

"It was buried in the mess that used to be your house."

And just when I thought things couldn't get any worse, he asked me if I would give the necklace to M—. He told me he had bought it for her after they broke up in hopes they would get back together.

I started crying again; my tears seemed to be habit-forming.

"I thought it was my birthday present. You promised to get me something special."

"And I did."

"Really?"

"Of course," he smiled with the confidence of a man who had found the perfect birthday gift. "I bought you a 'WHO DAT' Saints T-shirt with a fleur-de-lis on the back."

I knew full well that I should keep my mouth shut. Accusing a guy of not loving you enough was not the way to get him to love you more. But I was so damn mad about that "Who dat?" T-shirt that I could not think strategically.

"A single daisy picked from your grandmother's garden would have been about a hundred times better than giving me a football jersey for my sixteenth birthday."

"But you love the Saints."

"Everyone loves the Saints. That's not the point!" I yelled.

"Then what is the point?"

"You want the truth? Okay, fine then. You don't give a football jersey to a girl who's ready to take it, us—this thing we do—to the next level."

"I didn't even know we were on levels," he said, more depressed than ever. "For the last year I've been with M–. How could I be a thing with her and be on levels with you?"

"How could you be a thing with her and do this and that with those other girls?"

"It's not the same."

"Exactly. Because those other girls were just playing with you. I was dead serious."

Exhausted, I leaned back against the steps, further crushing what was left of my jeweled butterfly wings.

"Be careful with your wings," he said.

"Well, it's too damn late for that," I said, standing. "What really pisses me off is that while you were doing this and that with those other girls, you could have been doing this and that with me."

I turned and did the one thing I never ever thought I would or could do—the one thing I did not think I was capable of doing—I walked away. His words followed me.

"Those other girls didn't matter. But if I had done this or that with you, it would have counted."

I stopped. Despite all the monumental disappointments of the evening, I not only wanted him more than ever, I forgave him. That is how stupid love is. And I was knee-deep in it for sure.

But when I turned around to tell him so, once again, I was too late. Antwone was gone and Beano had returned, wide-eyed and disoriented.

"Are you okay?" I asked timidly.

He answered by puking all over his blue velvet slippers.

"I feel like the tail end of Fat Tuesday."

"It's been a rough night all the way around."

"What did he do this time?"

"I'll explain everything, but let's go inside and make a pot of coffee."

Folks in my daddy's bar are fond of saying, "Truth goes down better with whiskey." That may be so, but I've found lies are more easily crafted with black caffeine.

15.

I stayed up the rest of the night and well into the morning in The Betsy's kitchen, drinking chicory coffee with Beano and dodging his questions. He was a frantic mess.

"Please tell me we—or rather you and Antwone—did not do it."

"Do what?" I responded, playing dumb as a doormat.

"Go to the bone yard? Toss the salad? Did we get any kind of hinky?"

"All we did was talk. And that is the truth."

I ran my hand across the wooden tabletop, feeling the scars of a hundred years of use. Many a night and a story had been shared across this sturdy oak island.

"Did you tell him that he has to stop using my body as a hotel?"

Before I could concoct another lie, Beano stood and swept back his courtly coat dramatically.

"Did I or did I not do anything last night I would regret?"

"I swear all we did was talk," I answered quietly, avoiding the more startling revelations: the kiss with M— and his confession of love. Satisfied, Beano left for home to sleep the day away. He said it was exhausting enough just being Beano, but being him and Antwone was soul draining. I tried to hug him goodbye, but he pushed right past me and slammed the door behind him, the last of the guests to leave.

I looked at the kitchen clock; it was already past ten. Gina and The Betsy were upstairs, sleeping off the party. I wandered out of the kitchen into the dining room and surveyed the formidable messy aftermath. I grabbed an empty box tucked away in the closet under the stairs and began cleaning up. I figured I might as well make myself useful.

The Betsy wandered down the sweeping staircase at the civilized hour of noon. She was surprised to find me on the floor of the foyer following the trail of beads that had scattered from my broken wings the night before and picking them up one by one.

"It would be a lot easier to sweep those beads up with a broom," The Betsy said, exhaling the first drag of her morning cigarette.

"I'm doing penitence for everything I did and everything I did not do last night," I said, cornering an oblong turquoise bead stuck under the claw-foot Debusse console.

"Do tell, darling. Heaven may depend on penitence, but the devil is in the details and I want to hear a few," The Betsy said, assuming a regal position on her prized chaise lounge, which featured embossed monkeys dancing across a shiny, moonlit lake, their fabric faces clouded by time.

"I wouldn't even know where to start," I said, prying the bead loose and chasing it as it rolled across the uneven floor.

I went home an hour later, wrapped in Antwone's letterman jacket. Posted on the bar door was a glittery sign (penned by Miz Cocktail, no doubt) that stated the bar would be closed until five in observance of the Date of Commemoration, which was when some cardinal did the official math to let us know what was already on the calendar: the date of Fat Tuesday.

While the rest of New Orleans was taking down Christmas trees because everybody knows that to keep them up after Twelfth Night is bad luck, both the patrons and owners of the Cock's Comb were sleeping off a massive hangover. To open up the bar before dark would be foolhardy at best.

I slipped around to the alley entrance and unlocked the gate to the small patio, which separated the bar from the apartment, now littered with beer cans, liquor bottles, and cigarettes. Draped with beads and underwear, two potted plants had been uprooted. How that had happened I did not even want to know. As I made my way to the stairs, I maneuvered past four folks passed out on the wrought-iron patio furniture. Their arms and legs akimbo, two of them were nearly naked, all of them thankfully breathing. The outdoor heater, tilted but still standing, radiated a blanket of warmth that kept these four Twelfth Night revelers from freezing to death.

I crept into the apartment; my parents were still sound asleep. I could hear my father snoring. He sounded like a freight train, roaring 'round the bend.

I walked into my bedroom and was greeted by the only one who had missed me, King Oliver. He mewed in a whiny complaining tone as he wove around my ankles. Although streetwise, he was not really a bar kitty; the night had been hard on him.

Exhausted, I plopped down on the bed and did not fuss when King Oliver joined me, pouncing on my discarded wings. I scratched him behind both ears and whispered condolences as the two of us settled in for a long winter's nap. In my dreams, I was the one crowned queen of Twelfth Night. And it was me, not M—, whom Antwone took into his arms and kissed. And afterwards, we made a royal exit, sweeping up the grand staircase to the bedroom, where he drew a bath in Gina's claw-footed tub. Naked, we stepped into the water together.

I woke to my mother calling me from the kitchen and my cell phone DINGING incessantly. In true Mary Ellen fashion, she had managed to interrupt the sweetest of dreams.

"Camille, are you going to sleep the whole day away?"

I woke up angry and carried my mad into the kitchen where Mary Ellen was frying up thick slabs of bacon smothered in brown sugar. She called it praline bacon; my daddy called it heaven.

"What's the matter, honey? You look upset," my mother asked as I checked the messages on my cell. Beano had texted me about a gazillion times.

"Nothing," I lied.

"Well, it certainly sounds like something to me," Mary Ellen quipped.

"Do what you do best, Mother. Just leave me alone," I said bitterly. I never called her "Mother" and doing so now did not sit well with her. I grabbed Antwone's jacket and left before she could let me have it.

I scooted down the stairs, thankful that our overnight guests had packed up and left, taking their beads and panties with them. I closed the gate behind me and headed for Jackson Square to the Café du Monde. I found Beano sitting at an outside table under the green-and-white-ticked awning, on his second plate of beignets. I slid into a vintage 50s vinyl-backed chair across from him. He looked up peevishly.

"Well, you certainly took your sweet time. Didn't you get my message?"

"Which one?"

"The triple-911-get-your-butt-over-here one."

"Sorry," I said, reaching for one of his powdery donuts. He slapped my hand away.

"You lied to me," he said accusatorily. "You swore that HE didn't do anything that I would regret."

He reached into his backpack, pulled out his laptop, and slammed it open to his Facebook page, which was plastered with postings of the now infamous kiss. The latest photo was snapped just at the point when she was kissing him back, her mouth open and inviting. No question it was a kiss that carried a lot of collateral; a thousand words could not begin to do it justice.

"Well, I regret *this*," he said.

"It's just a kiss, Beano. A dare. Nothing to be ashamed of."

"I told Lewis I have never been attracted to girls."

"Tell him that it's human nature to experiment from time to time, especially during Mardi Gras. That's practically why the season was invented."

"He broke up with me."

You would think that at some point, I would cry myself out. But evidently, I had an unending supply because once again, I dissolved into tears as I considered how unfair life was. Beano's relationship, based on true and equal love, had been jeopardized for the sake of mine, which was based on a false premise. I tried to choke back a horrific sob that sounded like a cross between a guffaw and a mule hee-hawing, but I was unsuccessful. It was loud enough to draw attention from the noisy crowd.

"Oh here," Beano said, pushing his plate toward me. "You can have one of my beignets."

I managed to compose myself enough to take a bite of the deep-fried powdered-sugar dessert. It was the first thing I'd eaten in over twenty-four hours.

"Promise me that you will never summon Antwone into my body again."

"I can't. I don't always control his comings and goings. It's like bacon and eggs. Know what the difference is between the chicken and the pig at breakfast?"

"What?"

"The chicken is involved; the pig is committed. I'm like the chicken."

Beano was not amused. "Then who's the pig?"

"Would you feel any better if I told you that this would all be over by Ash Wednesday?"

"How can you know that?"

"Because the real Marie Laveau appeared to me at her grave and made me swear that I would give Antwone up for Lent. And you don't mess around with dead voodoo queens."

"I don't know. You might. I'm not sure I can trust you to keep your word, even if it was a sworn oath to a dead voodoo queen."

He was right about that. Truth was, I hadn't completely committed to giving Antwone up. I leaned over and planted a sugary kiss on Beano's forehead.

"I want my friend back," I whispered. "I miss the way we used to be."

"If you're serious about that, then you have to let *him* go. And you can start by giving M— his jacket," he said standing to leave.

On my way home, I stopped in St. Louis Cathedral, seeking guidance. Only three other lost souls sought sanctuary in the chapel that Sunday evening, and one was sleeping. I walked down the nave toward the altar but before I reached the crucifix at the chancel, I made a dramatic left turn to the epistle side of the church. I lit a candle at the feet of St. Joseph and silently made my request: the wisdom to know what to do.

I lingered under the canopy of candles, waiting for some kind of epiphany. When none came, I left the warm sanctuary for the chilly night. I paused to take in the whole of Jackson Square's flickering lights of promise, none of them meant for me.

"I'm not hungry. I ate with Beano," I said to Mary Ellen as I plowed through the kitchen where she was clearly waiting for me.

"Not so fast," Mary Ellen said, standing. "You forgot to lock the gate again."

"Sorry, I'll be more careful."

"This isn't like the garage at the old place, Camille. We've already been broken into once. I don't want it to happen again."

"I said I was sorry."

"There's one more thing before you disappear into your room," she said, lifting my chin so that we were eye to eye. "I wanna show you something."

She gestured for me to sit with her at the table. On top was the old metal suitcase that had made it through our exile and back again. Inside were papers and old family documents. She opened a yellowed envelope and gingerly pulled out a tattered photograph.

"Your great-grandmother came to Texas in 1919, all alone, a young widow with a small baby. We found this in her house after she died. I think it's a photograph of my grandfather."

"You think? You mean you don't know?" I asked as she handed the photo to me.

"She wouldn't talk about him except to say that he died in the great flu epidemic that swept the country the year before she came to Texas. Every time we asked, she'd say it was just too painful to discuss."

I looked down at the well-worn photo and saw a handsome, young, light-skinned Black man in a white linen suit, smiling back at me.

"We searched for records of him, but we never even found a marriage certificate. Probably because there hadn't been one. Interracial marriage was illegal back then, which would explain why she didn't want us to know that she had chosen to love a man who could never be the legal father of her child."

"Do you even know his name?"

"No. All I know for sure is that my mother had his eyes."

"Certainly explains my hair."

"Yes, it does."

A million thoughts swirled through my head. Her waiting so long to share this important piece of information with me was like telling someone they're adopted after they're all grown up. Knowing your roots doesn't necessarily change your present, but it does help explain the past. And now I had to reconsider mine. I never felt particularly connected to my Texas relatives, partly because my own mother seemed to have so little use for them. But at that moment I felt a kinship to the great-grandmother I barely knew. And not just because we had both fallen in love with men of color, but because we had both suffered through a love cut short unfairly—mine by an untimely death, hers by an unjust law.

"Why did you wait so long to tell me?"

"I don't know. I guess I wanted to make sure you were old enough to handle it."

"You shouldn't have kept it from me."

"You're right." She reached over and stroked the arm of Antwone's storm-stained jacket. "I know now how much you loved him. And I'm sorry for the things I said and what I didn't say."

"It's okay, Momma. It's behind us now."

"You haven't called me Momma since you were three."

"Well, enjoy it. 'Cause you might have to wait another decade or two to hear it again."

She laughed and reached out to hug me. I leaned in, melting into her open arms. In that tender moment, St. Joseph answered my prayer. I found wisdom not in the house of God, but in my mother's kitchen. I knew what I had to do. It would not be easy, but for the good of all of us, I had to take this first step in the process of letting go.

As soon as I closed the door to my bedroom, I called Gina. Because I knew I would need her help.

16.

The next morning, I woke up earlier than usual, dressed in the dark, grabbed Antwone's jacket, skipped breakfast, and hurried out the door. When I reached the bus stop in Jackson Square, I felt eyes on me, but since I had been so skittish lately, I blew it off. I got on the bus and rode to what used to be our school, now a ratty collection of trailers and portables. The bus doors swooshed open and I stepped out onto the cracked pavement.

Gina was waiting for me outside the trailer that served as our first period English class, carrying a thermos of coffee and a paper bag with two croissants spread with deviled ham. Even though it was cloudy, she wore dark glasses to hide her "naked eyes." Gina never left the house without putting on two pounds of mascara and eyeliner.

Inside the trailer, Gina poured the coffee while I walked over to M—'s assigned desk. I slipped the jacket off my shoulders and hugged it tight to my chest. It felt like I was giving up a piece of him.

"You've come this far, Camille. Don't stop now," Gina urged.

I took a deep breath and then hung the jacket on the back of M—'s chair. I opened my backpack, pulled out a sheet of engraved stationery embossed with my initials, and sat down to compose a letter. Gina handed me a cup of steaming coffee as I struggled with the words. "I don't want her to think that I'm giving in to her. I want her to understand that my sacrifice comes from a place of strength, not weakness."

"How about 'Here's his jacket, bitch!'" Gina offered.

"Close," I said. "But not quite."

I spent a good half hour composing the letter, with Gina growing more impatient by the minute. Finally, I put my pen down and read the note aloud.

"Dear M–, I found his jacket for you. And although we will never know for sure who he would want to wear it, I think you should have it for as long your love lasts. C–"

I had never signed my name with just a C and a dash, but I liked the way it looked on expensive paper. It connected the beginning salutation to the signature end with natural symmetry. I folded the note and as I placed it in the envelope, the same uneasy feeling I had when I was getting on the bus washed over me. Somebody was spying on me. I turned quickly and thought I saw a reflection of a man staring at me in the window.

I ran out of the room to investigate, circled the trailer, and looked down the breezeway, but there was no sign of anyone. A cold chill swept over me, not like a wintery wind but a chill in the bones that comes from the inside out. Was my uneasy feeling Antwone signaling his return or something more sinister? I folded my arms across my chest to warm my hands. A few minutes later, Gina emerged from the trailer. She threw away the remains of our breakfast in a nearby trash bin and tossed me my backpack.

"What the hell, Camille? You always leave me to clean up the mess."

"Let's skip morning classes," I said.

"Aren't you in enough trouble with Sister Mary Benedict already?"

"Possibly," I said. "But you know how M– is when she gets what she wants. How she acts all superior. I can't do that today."

Gina agreed to skip school, but only if we did something really decadent, which wasn't a problem because in New Orleans, doing decadent was easy.

Back in the Quarter and over a shared plate of French toast, dusted with powdered sugar and smothered in maple syrup, we decided to get tattoos. It was my first, but Gina already had three, none that showed. The Betsy was opposed to tattoos in general but she believed that if a lady were to indulge in body art, it should be situated in a spot where only your lover could see. Which made me wonder if she herself might be harboring a little ink in some secret place.

When it came my turn, I knew exactly what I wanted. A single letter in Lucinda Calligraphy with a bobcat emerging from the center loop as if it were launching itself into the world, just like the insignia on Antwone's letterman jacket. I made one change. Instead of using the letter "B" for St. Bede's, I had the tattoo artist carve the letter "A" in the small of my back to honor my lost love.

"I think this 'letting go' process of yours just took one permanent step backwards," Gina commented as the artist finished his handiwork.

We made it back to St Bede's by noon and slipped into the portable that served as the lunchroom. While we were deciding where to sit, I felt a tap on my shoulder. I turned around and standing in front of me and surrounded by her girls was M–. She faced me down with a cold, hard stare.

"What's up?" I asked.

She slapped me hard across the face. The entire lunchroom quieted, because even though there were half a dozen private dramas going on at various tables, none could match mine.

"What the hell, M–?" I winced.

"I've known you were crazy for a long time. But what you did is beyond messed up."

"I gave you the jacket—just like you asked. I'm trying to make peace."

"If this is how you make peace, it's gonna be a long war."

M– signaled her cheerleader buddy Charmaine, who stepped forward, carrying what was left of Antwone's jacket. She handed it to M– who held it up for all of St. Bede's to see. It had been sliced to shreds, ravaged by a knife, and the embroidered letter had been carved out, leaving a hole in the heart of the jacket.

"Oh my god, who would do a thing like that?"

"I'm thinking—YOU, bitch!"

"I could never, ever destroy what belonged to him."

Gina pushed her way into the crowd. "I was there with Camille and I swear to you she did not do this. When we left, the jacket was in one piece."

"Gina's right. We were together the entire time except when I ran outside the trailer."

M— stewed over this new information. "So what you're saying is that you left *her* alone with the jacket?"

"Way to throw me under the bus, Camille," Gina whispered hoarsely to me.

"I should have known it was you, Va-*gina*, because you're an even bigger skank than Camille."

Well, that did it. Gina could blow off being called a skank, but under no circumstances could anyone make fun of her name. It was kinda like my hair; we were both sensitive on those respective subjects.

"Girl fight!" William Renfro yelled as Gina headbutted M— in the stomach. They fell to the floor, clawing at each other, pulling hair and clothes. The teacher on lunchroom duty ran out of the room to fetch Sister Benedict. She wasn't about to get tangled up in a girl-fight mess.

They crashed into a table; half-eaten lunches splattered all over them. I tried to separate them, but M—'s grip was so strong that she left marks on Gina's arm as dark and deep as my new tattoo. Beano joined in to help and somehow we were able to pry them apart, just as Sister Benedict the "Enforcer" barged into the lunchroom. She took one look at the knocked over tables and food carnage and turned to the two girls, both breathing hard.

"What's been going on in here?" Sister Benedict asked, peering over her wire-rimmed glasses.

"Armageddon," William offered.

After a quick sorting out of details and accusations, Sister

Benedict ordered Gina, M–, and me to her office for further interrogation. Gina and M– were singled out because they had been fighting, and I was called in on general principles. I watched helplessly as Charmaine tossed the remains of Antwone's jacket into the trash.

Sister Benedict was an astute woman. To say I was involved was the understatement of the year. I accepted that the entire lunchroom debacle was my fault. I was the vortex of the tornado, the eye of the hurricane, the center of the storm. But what I didn't understand was how all my good intentions had become so cosmically mishandled. How could it be that even when I tried to do the right thing, it turned out wrong?

Suspended for three days, I took my time getting home. I meandered through the narrow cobblestone streets of the Quarter, with what was left of Antwone's jacket. I had retrieved it from the lunchroom dumpster and stuffed it into my backpack, its water-stained sleeves now marked with ketchup and grease. I wondered if my mother's cleaner in Metairie could salvage it. Or if it, like my reputation, was beyond repair.

It was almost seven and already dark when I reached the Cock's Comb. I entered through the back to avoid facing the inevitable—my parents. I reached the side yard and started to enter the combination on the lock, but I noticed the gate was ajar. I was pretty sure I had locked it when I left that morning, but since I had royally screwed up in every other way, I figured my disaster of a day probably began with my leaving the back gate open again.

As I entered the courtyard, I could hear King Oliver, purring contently. I followed the sounds to the steps where my cat was curled up next to the missing insignia from Antwone's letterman jacket, left in plain sight for me to find. At that moment, I realized the eyes I had felt watching me early this morning must have belonged to *him*. He followed me to school and used the knife that had briefly been mine to destroy Antwone's jacket. And he left its carved-out heart on the steps as a warning of some sorts. A threat meant just for me.

꙳

"Tell her, Donald. Tell her what *we* decided," my mother announced at breakfast the next morning.

Mary Ellen put a lot of emphasis on the "we" lest I think she was running the show. But the look on my daddy's face told a different story. I could tell he was not fully on board with "their" decision.

"Your mother—correction, your mother and I—had a long talk with Sister Benedict, who told us you have moved beyond your own problems to become a real disruptive influence on others. She said any more trouble from you and she'd ask you to leave St. Bede's."

"Okay, I get it. I'll straighten up. Get my act together. Fly right. All that," I said, aware that I sounded insincere.

"Sister Benedict also suggested that it wasn't completely your fault," Mary Ellen said. "She blamed us, too, for not providing enough supervision and real consequences to your acting out."

I did not like the turn this conversation was taking. "I'm not acting out. I'm reacting. There's a difference."

"Not to Sister Benedict," my daddy said.

"Okay, so we'll all do better," I said, standing to leave.

"Sit down, young lady," my mother said.

"You mean there's more?"

"Your mother and I agreed that we can't ignore what happened in the lunchroom."

"We're seriously worried about what you're going to do next," my mother chimed in.

"Like what?"

"I don't know. Skip school again. Start doing drugs. Get a tattoo."

I cringed. She saw. "Oh no, are you doing drugs?"

"No, of course not. But if we're being honest here and I think we should be, I did get a tattoo."

My mother looked like she was about to pass out.

"It's not that big of a deal. Besides, it's my body."

"Yes, it is. And your *body* is grounded."

"For how long?" I asked.

My daddy cleared his throat; the words did not come out easy. "For the entire of Mardi Gras."

"What!" I screamed like a wounded animal. "You can't do that to me. You don't understand."

Mary Ellen shook her head. "We understand plenty. We're done blaming your bad behavior on the storm or living over a bar or going to school in a FEMA trailer. It's time you take responsibility for your actions."

I couldn't believe the hypocrisy of it all. My parents had raised me with a free hand. Now suddenly they became the parental equivalent of the Gestapo. My computer was blocked from social sites in an attempt to cut me off from friends who might be influencing my bad behavior. What they didn't know was denying me access to social media was not that big of a deal because I had no friends left to text or call. After his breakup with Lewis, Beano managed to get transferred out of the one class we shared together because he didn't even want to be in the same room with me.

While Beano punished me with silence, Gina struck her blows with words. She wrote me a lengthy text five bubbles long in which she essentially broke up with me because she couldn't handle our reversed roles: me being crazier than her. I had built my whole world around the advantages of having two best friends. And now I had lost them both.

So while the rest of New Orleans engaged in one giant city-wide block party, I was held prisoner in my own room. Sometimes I would open my window to the winter cold and hear the faint sounds of marching bands somewhere in the distance, ushering in the next krewe, the next parade. I could only imagine the brightly colored floats and flying plastic beads rolling down the city streets.

Trying to let go of Antwone hadn't worked out so well. I decided that if the universe was plotting against me, I might as well give in to magic. I swore to myself that if I felt that familiar tug from the other side manifested in a shudder or chill—which I was now convinced was a cosmic sign of Antwone entering Beano's body—that I would break down the bars of my prison room and escape. Whatever the cost, I would find him.

17.

With the clock to Mardi Gras ticking down to three weeks, I grew more and more despondent. But on Saturday morning, Mary Ellen announced that our old neighbor, Adele, had invited us to watch the Krewe du Vieux parade from the balcony of her sister's apartment on Royal.

"Who's gonna look after the bar?" I asked, looking up from my cheesy grits.

"Miz Cocktail has volunteered," Donald said.

"Who's going to look after me?"

"I think you can manage to stay out of trouble for a few hours," Mary Ellen said.

I couldn't stand the thought of missing the parade. I'd been going to it since I was two, even though a lot of parents wouldn't let their young kids within an inch of it because the floats are so, well, sexual. But not my daddy. He said parents who wouldn't let their kids see the Krewe du Vieux were sexually repressed idiots.

"If the whole family was invited, aren't they going to wonder why your 'Mardi Gras baby' didn't come along? I hate to think about you explaining to Adele and all her high-minded friends how you raised some kind of juvenile delinquent," I said, casual as can be.

"Maybe it's time to loosen up a bit," my daddy said to my mother, clearly leaving the decision to her. "She has been as good as gold. But whatever you think is best."

My mother sighed; she weighed her options carefully.

"Well, I guess enough is enough. If your father is sure it would be okay, you can come along to the parade."

"Hallelujah," he answered.

We gathered early, over fifty of us, an hour before the festivities started. Even the unseasonably cold weather could not dampen my spirits. While the adults were getting liquored up on Adele's version of a familiar New Orleans cocktail, which she renamed the "Storm of the Century Hurricane," I slipped out to reserve a place on the balcony at the front of the railing. Since I was short, I had to secure a spot early on to see and be seen. I shouted out, "Bon Mardi Gras!" and waved to the enormous crowd below like I was the Queen of Something Else. A group of drunk college-age guys waved back and the ginger among them shouted, "Show us your titties!"

"You wanna a show? Take yourself over to Bourbon. 'Cause you'll get none of that here," I yelled back and then added good-naturedly, "unless you have some really good throw beads to toss my way!"

By the time the parade meandered its way down our street, our balcony was weighted down with way too many people, all of them but me drunk on booze and stories. My parents were not among them. Donald had been waylaid into helping Adele make all those fancy cocktails and my mother stayed to keep him company.

On the street below, marchers threw doubloons to the gathering crowds. A crazy float with Barbie and Ken dolls representing various post-Katrina politicians in compromising sexual positions rounded the corner. It looked like second graders with very dirty adult minds had made it.

On the next float were two huge naked papier-mâché women named after hurricanes Katrina and Rita and engaged in lesbian sex. Our balcony shook with laughter at the sight. Pushed against the wrought-iron railing, I swore I saw Beano on the sidewalk, standing behind a tall, thin woman with pale pink hair swirled on top of her head like cotton candy. I leaned over the balcony and hollered out his name, but before he could answer, a strand of octagon-shaped, deep purple beads slammed into my face and nearly ripped out my right eye. I cried out, but nobody could hear me over the big brass band following the float. Pressed against the rail, I started to tumble over when a shudder passed through me and I heard a voice calling out from the crowd, "Don't be afraid, baby girl. I got you."

My eyes were watering so bad that I could barely see what my heart already knew. Down in the street below, a young Black man held out his arms to catch me if I fell.

I threw caution to the wind and, with a leg over the balcony, prepared to launch myself into the street. The crowd below cheered my daring. I dropped down and grabbed the railing cap, but just as I was about to let go, a super-sized jester grabbed my wrists.

"I got you," he said, trying to lift me on the balcony.

"No, let go. My boyfriend's down there," I said.

Antwone held out his arms and the crowd around him joined in, chanting, "Let her go. Let her go. Let her go."

"Please, mister," I begged. "I got to see him tonight."

There was a moment of hesitation.

"Oh hell, to be young and in love on a night like this. Hang on till I say when."

He leaned over the balcony, dropping me as low as he could and after one "Hail Mary," he released me.

Like a rock star launched into a mosh pit, I dropped into a sea of outstretched arms who carried me across the crowd straight into the arms of my dead boyfriend, who smiled as he lifted me high above his head. Pressed together by the bodies surrounding us, he slid me down to the ground. My feet touched the street, light as a feather. The Mardi Gras groundlings cheered my arrival into their midst. Antwone embraced me and kissed me hard. Kissed me for real. This time like he meant it. The crowd roared its approval. From the balcony, the relieved jester crossed himself and blew us kisses, just like the Franciscan priest from *Romeo and Juliet*. We laughed out loud and then Antwone whispered in my ear, "You seen enough of the parade?"

I nodded and he took my hand, leading the way. I followed him through the crowded street, and we slipped into an empty alleyway. We were both slightly breathless.

"You okay?" he asked, stroking my face.

I nodded and reached up to kiss him once more. But this time, he cut the kiss short, ending on a gentle note. Afraid that the memory of M— was subconsciously coming between us, I blurted out my deepest concerns.

"I know you have a problem being with a white girl, but you might try to be a little less prejudiced. Since I'm the only one who can see you. Who can hear you. Who you can kiss and who can actually kiss you back. And not that I want to win you over on a technicality but as it turns out, my great-grandfather was probably Black, which makes me..." I struggled to find the words, "less white."

Antwone laughed out loud. "Baby girl, we are way beyond color. We got bigger fish to fry." He turned serious. "I don't know how long I have. But there are things I have to tell you."

"What's wrong?" I asked.

"I don't know. You in trouble?"

"Lately, all the time."

"You know what I mean. Somebody after you?"

"Maybe. I don't know for sure."

"Who?"

"That man from the alley. Why are you asking all these questions?"

"Something bad is gonna happen. I feel it."

"Something bad has already happened. What could be worse than what we've been through already?"

"There's always something worse. Don't you know that by now? And whatever it is, it's getting closer. Breathing down our necks. That much I know."

It occurred to me that Antwone had become the Spy Boy he aspired to be, an otherworldly presence at the front of the tribe alerting the rest of us to approaching trouble.

A loud roar from the parade crowd echoed through the alley, followed by an eerie silence. We stepped back into the street to see what had hushed the carnival crowd. Antwone was tall enough to see over their heads, but I was not, so he lifted me up onto his shoulders to witness the tail end of the parade. With a clear view, I could see what had brought the rowdy street to a standstill.

The last float of the parade was completely empty, like the riderless horse following the casket in a funeral procession, honoring the many victims of Katrina. On the side was painted: "We celebrate life, we mourn the past, we shall never forget."

Antwone lowered me into his arms. I looked into his eyes and whispered, "That float was for you."

We kissed a third time, a lingering and closed-mouth kiss. I read once that the endorphins produced by kissing are 200 times more powerful than morphine. Ancient lovers believed that a kiss could unite two souls because the spirit was carried in one's breath. It was that kind of kiss, full of sadness, gentleness, and intimacy.

When I opened my eyes, Antwone once more had left me and in his place was Beano, more terrified than he'd ever been before. His body literally convulsed with tremors from Antwone's exit. He pushed me away with trembling hands.

"Stay away from me. I can't do this anymore."

He took off. I ran after and grabbed his arm. "Please, let me explain. This was kind of a cosmic emergency."

His face softened and he pleaded so earnestly it gave me pause. "I've had enough. The game you and your dead boyfriend are playing is killing me."

I released my grip and let Beano go, just like the harlequin jester had let me drop from the balcony. He disappeared into the shadows of the night.

Despite the rocky encounter with Beano, a strange peace settled over me on Sunday that extended into Monday morning and followed me to school. Marie Laveau had brought Antwone back to me twice now, certain to be followed by many more visits. Time enough to contemplate how and when I would have to give him up for good. But for now, I looked forward to more stolen moments and many more kisses.

I stepped into first period English, slid into my desk, and began doodling in my notebook about voodoo queens and lovers' trysts. A tap on my desk woke me from my reverie and I looked up to see Gina standing in front of me.

"You've really done it now," she said with contempt.

"What are you talking about?"

"You don't know?"

"Know what?"

"Beano's left town. He up and moved away Sunday morning. His grandmother won't say where. Just that he had to get away from you."

I was totally blindsided. My boyfriend's ability to enter my best friend's body had intensified of late, but I worried that distance could make a spirit visitation impossible. I had to do something and quick.

At lunch, I called his grandmother to sweet-talk her into telling me where he was. Roselle Benoit was a fifth-generation New Orleanian born and bred, but she was willing to ignore the Texas side of my family tree because she liked me. In fact, we had been almost-friends once upon a time before all of our lives turned inside out.

"Hi, Miz Benoit," I said cheerfully when she answered. "This is Camille."

She hung up on me. After she slammed down the phone for the fourth time, I should have stopped, but like an annoying telemarketer, I kept calling.

On the eighth attempt, she finally picked up but before I could get two words out, she interrupted. "Camille, I know you have been a good friend to my grandson, but I'm begging you to leave him alone. He's not doing well. His grades are dropping. He's not sleeping. At first, I thought it was natural—we've all been to hell and back—but Sunday morning he said the storm had nothing to do with it. He said he had lost his center, the core of who he was, and that he couldn't be around you anymore."

"But he can't go back to living with his stepmom. He was miserable before."

"He didn't. My Langley and his uppity wife moved back east just before Christmas. Didn't Beano tell you?"

He had not. But I was not surprised.

"Katrina was her breaking point," Roselle said. "She gave my son an ultimatum. It was either her or New Orleans. He chose her and they packed up Kemper and moved to Cambridge. Personally, I think he made the wrong choice."

"I couldn't agree more."

"Look, if Beano doesn't pull himself together, I'll lose him too. Swear to me that you will leave him alone."

It was my turn to hang up on her. I could make no such promise.

That afternoon when I got home from school, I logged on to his Facebook page for clues. But he was one step ahead of me. He had shut down his account altogether. And then it dawned on me that maybe he had gone to stay with his cousins in the bayou. I racked my brain trying to remember their last name but came up blank.

I called Cousin Jeanette who prided herself on knowing everybody who was anybody in the entire parish. After a brief exchange of family news, I asked her if she knew any Benoits who had married into one of the local families.

"Well, let me think," she said. In the background, I heard the clunk of a metal spoon against a pot in a steady beat as she stirred. Cousin Jeanette was always cooking up something, including excuses.

"I swear, Camille, I can't think of a single body who married a Benoit from New Orleans. Unless, of course, well, if this is one of your colored friends, then I wouldn't know anything about that."

For the second time that day, I hung up the phone on somebody's mother.

Beano was gone. And I had no idea where he was. Far away, his grandmother said. Far from danger. Far from New Orleans. Far from me.

18.

Even though my parents granted me an early parole, I essentially re-grounded myself. I lost more weight and retreated to my room, missing five back-to-back parades that rolled under cloudy, damp skies. Early Sunday morning I visited the grave of my dead voodoo queen and prayed that she would give Antwone the strength to make it home to me, no matter how many miles separated us.

But unlike the last time, Marie Laveau did not appear. No swirling mist, no voice from beyond the grave, just stone-cold silence. I began to wonder if I had imagined the whole thing. Maybe I wasn't crazy in love. Maybe I was just plain crazy. It was a theory worth considering.

"I can tell you right now, we are worried sick about her," I heard Mary Ellen say as her footsteps approached my closed bedroom door on Lundi Gras, the Monday before Fat Tuesday. I was, as I had been for weeks, alone in my room.

Mary Ellen continued as the footsteps drew nearer.

"She hasn't been herself since we came back. Even carnival season hasn't lifted her spirits. But I'm sure hoping a visit from you will cheer her right up."

The door creaked slowly open and standing before me was a sight for sore eyes. Bama leaned her cane against the doorjamb and opened her arms, inviting me in. I jumped off my bed and ran to her. Her arms closed around me, and she swallowed me up whole.

"Child, what have they been feeding you? Rabbit food? 'Cause you're so skinny, I bet you have to stand up twice to even cast a shadow. You come on out with your Bama and I'll see to it you have something real to eat, something that'll put a little meat on those bones."

We took the bus uptown to a joint called Voodoo Barbecue and shared a magnificent meal of pulled pork, sweet potato soufflé, and collard greens with bacon drippings. I ate like I hadn't had anything to eat in weeks, which in fact was close to the truth. As I dug into my second helping of white chocolate bread pudding, she told me what brought her home.

"'Bout a month ago, I got a letter from a young man, a Spy Boy for one of the tribes, asking for a photo of my late husband in his Big Chief finery. He remembered seeing Tito as a little boy and he wanted to copy some of the designs for his own father's Big Chief collar.

"That young man lost almost his whole family—his momma, his grandma, and three brothers—to the water. He said that after the last funeral, the one for his baby brother, his daddy holed up in their FEMA trailer. Sometimes he drank. Mostly he slept. 'Bout a month ago, the son finally coaxed his daddy out of that dark place, and together they began the beadwork for his Mardi Gras collar. They started so late, he had no idea if they would finish in time.

"I can't tell you how much his letter touched me. Anyways, I did him one better than a picture. I sent him the real collar my husband wore. And I promised him that I'd be down in the Treme so I could see his Spy Boy self whooping, hollering, and announcing his Big Chief Daddy to the other tribes. I knew it wouldn't be easy to come home, but if this young man, having lost so much, could dance his way through it, how could I stay away?"

"I'm sure it will mean a lot to him for you to be there."

"I'm just one old woman. But we all do what we can do. Ain't that so?"

"Some of us do more than others," I said.

"Will you do something for me?" she asked.

I nodded solemnly, knowing that whatever she wanted, I would not be able to refuse.

"Will you help me plan Antwone's funeral?" she asked quietly and then added, "It still bothers me that we don't have his body, but I know the time has come to put his soul to rest."

"I might be able to help you with that," I said, putting down my spoon. I was no longer hungry.

We rode the bus back to the church lady's house where she was staying. After dropping her off, I walked through Woldenburg Park where the storied African American krewe, Zulu, was putting on a festival like no other. Part pep rally, part spiritual revival, Lundi Gras was more than the day before Fat Tuesday; it was its own celebration. Even though the crowd was sparse compared to other years, spirits were high. On center stage, a singer belted out an old favorite, the upbeat "Mardi Gras Mambo."

The roar of a U.S. Coast Guard cutter docking at the riverbank drowned his song out. A cheer rose up from the crowd as former Zulu Kings in all their feathered finery walked off the boat into their midst.

But neither the upbeat music nor the beautiful weather could raise my spirits. My mood hung over the bacchanalia like a dark fog. It followed me home as I left the street party and moved with the surging crowds through the Quarter.

When I arrived, I found Lewis waiting for me outside the bar, looking about as uncomfortable as a whore in church.

"Well, this is a surprise. What brings you to the Quarter?"

"Beano called last night," he said simply.

I quickly ushered him through the bar and into the empty courtyard so that we could talk. Nervously, Lewis fumbled with his crooked collar, trying to get it to lay down straight.

"He says he wants to get back together. We talked and stuff for hours. I'm not lying. It got pretty intense."

From the way Lewis acted, I could only assume that the call culminated in some pretty amazing phone sex.

"What did he say?" I asked.

"That he loved me," Lewis said.

"He does," I said.

"That's what my psychic said. I had a reading this afternoon and according to the tea leaves, Beano never cheated on me."

"He didn't."

"The psychic saw something else," Lewis said. His coal-black eyes narrowed at me. "He said that you were the only one who knew the whole story, who could quote 'unravel his deception.' Look, I know you don't like me much—"

"That's not true. Or not exactly true. All that really matters is that Beano loves you."

"Then why did he kiss M— and tell her he loved her?"

I was so tired of telling lies that I decided to tell the truth. Besides, I figured he wouldn't believe me anyway.

"It wasn't him," I said.

"What do you mean?"

"I mean when Beano kissed M—, he wasn't in control of his faculties."

"I know. He was drunk. If he's bi-, just tell me."

"Oh, Lewis, if Beano were the last man on earth, he still wouldn't do a woman."

"Then why did he do M—?"

"He didn't. It was Antwone."

"Antwone? Dead Antwone?"

"Yep."

"That's insane."

"Pretty much."

Lewis paced as I laid out the timeline of each possession. When I finished, he shook his head in measured disbelief.

"Even when I thought he had lied to me, I didn't stop loving him. I couldn't if I wanted to."

For the first time, I began to admire his character, and even allowed myself to like him, just a little bit.

"You know where he is?"

Lewis looked away, avoiding eye contact.

"But you have a number for him, right?"

Lewis nodded.

"Give me your cell."

I don't know why but he did. I found Beano's number in recent contacts and hit redial. He answered on the third ring, a record for even him.

"Do not hang up on me," I started. "Hear me out. Please come home tomorrow because Lewis has things to say to you that can't be said over the phone. Things that shouldn't have to wait. And it's my last chance to say the things I need to say to Antwone. To set things right. You have to come back for Mardi Gras. Because there are people here who need and love you. Swear to me that you won't let us down."

He hung up without a word.

"Well, what did he say?" Lewis asked anxiously.

"I think he's coming," I answered, hoping that Beano's love for Lewis was stronger than his fear of me.

I grabbed his arm as he started to leave. "Text me when he gets here, okay?"

"I'll do my best," Lewis said, leaving me alone in the court-yard with nothing but hope to keep me company.

I got up at four-thirty the next morning, unwrapped the special crème Aisha concocted for me, and began the arduous process of straightening my hair. Two hours later, I rinsed my hair and blew it dry. It came out straight as a board and about six inches longer. With one last satisfied look in the mirror, I walked into the kitchen where my daddy was packing up an ice chest with sandwiches and beer. His jaw about dropped to his knees when he saw my new hairdo.

"Good lord, Camille, you don't even look like yourself."

Well, he was one to talk. Decked out in his Fat Tuesday regalia—purple Afro, gold lamé shirt, and green polka-dot clown pants—he was a real Mardi Gras mess. I, on the other hand, was dressed head to toe in black: jeans, sweater, and boots.

"Aren't you going to mask this year?" he asked.

"I am costumed," I said. "I decided to go as a white girl with regular hair."

"Good enough. I've got the cooler. You grab the butterfly net. 'Cause we want to be in a good spot when Zulu rolls down Jackson. Your mother will meet up with us later at Rex."

Zulu always rolled first, around eight, before Rex made its own way down a similar route mid-morning, at a time more convenient for my mother.

Still, Zulu was my favorite, and it was tradition for my daddy and me to go together. We each had a thermos of coffee—his laced with bourbon—the big ice chest with food for later, and most importantly, the butterfly net. We pushed our way to a corner on Canal and set up camp. Waiting for the parade to begin, I texted Lewis for the third time that morning, asking if Beano had shown up.

He texted back: *Stop already. Will text when I have something to say.*

"Grab the net and climb up on that chest, Camille. Zulu's about to roll!" Donald shouted, jump-starting his day with a swig of jacked-up coffee.

A slew of marchers dressed in fright wigs and grass skirts strutted by, all in blackface, just like in the old-timey minstrel shows, except the blackfaced marchers in Zulu were Black themselves, not white. Zulu is hard to explain to an outsider. Seeing it for the first time is like watching a really old film from the fifties on how to avoid racial stereotypes.

We were swept up in a swarm of people all clamoring for one of the most prized Mardi Gras throws, the golden nugget, a decorated coconut handed, not thrown, to a few lucky parade watchers. Donald and I hadn't snagged a coconut since I was in middle school, but this year, he attached a long pole to the butterfly net to give us an advantage. I yelled myself hoarse, pleading with marchers to put a coconut in my net. I had grown desperate by the time the last float rolled by. It was fronted by "Big Shot Zulu," a thirty-foot papier-mâché blackfaced man in a white derby and suit, holding a stogie that was about the same size as me. I zeroed in on one of float's marchers, made eye contact, and pleaded my case.

"Please, mister, I need me some good luck juju."

He jumped off the float and hand-delivered that nugget to me. With a tip of his hat and a sideways smile, he left me with these parting words. "*Bon mardi gras.*"

"Well, that was easy," my daddy said with just the right amount of irony as he admired my prize throw. After all, it had only taken us five years of yelling and pleading to snag just one.

We wandered down the street to our customary spot to wait for Rex. Everybody on our side of the street either knew each other or knew somebody who knew somebody. Everybody was asking the same question. "How did you do?" And we all knew what they meant.

"The bus took me and my three children from the Dome to the Causeway where we spent two days on the overpass before they got us out," said a woman in oversized Mardi Gras glasses, corralling her three rambunctious kids.

I remembered the faces of families I'd seen on the news after the storm, begging for water, for food, for someone to care, and imagined hers had been among them. And yet here she was today laughing with her kids.

"Look who I found," Mary Ellen said, pushing through the crowd. "My god, Gina, it seems like we haven't seen you in forever. How's your momma?"

Wrapped in gold tulle, her hair dyed Mardi Gras green, Gina was held hostage in my mother's embrace.

I wanted to grab Gina myself and either hug her or slap her silly, but I was paralyzed by all my prior bad behavior. Luckily, she spoke first.

"I'm tired of being mad at you," Gina said. "It takes way too much energy. What are you up to later?"

"Just hanging out. Seeing where the day takes me."

Waiting for Lewis to text me. To see Beano. To be with Antwone. But I didn't tell her any of that.

Gina begged me to come to her house where The Betsy was staging a big to-do, with live music from one of the brass bands that marched in Rex. I checked my cell. Still no word from Lewis.

So I said yes to a party in the Garden District. The place was jammed when we got there. Everybody who thought they were anybody in New Orleans was either dancing in the backyard or drinking at the bar. Gina snagged us a couple of daiquiris unnoticed.

I tried to lose myself in the party; I danced with old men and young women. I sang along to the big brass band and stuffed myself on crawfish étouffée. And continued to check my cell every five minutes.

As dusk settled over the city and twinkle lights cast a glow on the remaining revelers, The Betsy pulled me aside to a dark corner of the backyard so she could sneak a cigarette.

"You've lost weight," The Betsy said, eyeing my diminished frame.

"I don't know how," I said. "I eat like a horse."

"Well, nothing burns calories like unrequited love. Have there been any more visitations?" she asked nonchalantly, like she was ordering a pizza from Angeli on Decatur.

"I was hoping to see him today," I answered. "But I have no idea where to find him."

"Where does your heart tell you to go?"

I closed my eyes and listened. "I feel drawn to the Quarter."

"Then go already," she said, smiling her approval.

Before I left, I found Gina in the foyer to tell her goodbye.

"I have a bad feeling about your leaving," she said. "Stay and spend the night."

She told me that The Betsy had shared the mystical turn in my life with her the day before, hoping it would soften her feelings toward me and lead to our reconciliation. She didn't quite buy into the "whole body possession thing." But her skepticism of the supernatural did not prevent her from worrying about the real-world danger of my being alone in the Quarter on Fat Tuesday. I tried to reassure her.

"I promise not to do anything you wouldn't do," I said.

"If that's supposed to make me feel better, you have not succeeded," she said.

"Maybe this will," I said, retrieving my prized token, the decorated Zulu coconut, from the console and giving it to her. She threw her arms around my neck.

"I love you," she said.

"I love you back," I said, hugging her hard.

An odd feeling of finality swept over me like a wave; it felt like I was telling her goodbye.

On the bus back to the Quarter, I texted Lewis and told him where I would be. I got off at Basin Street, avoiding Bourbon because that's where all the tourists go to get drunk, throw up, and be obnoxious and I didn't need any of that. I headed for Royal instead where I ran into Miz Cocktail, who was wearing a black corset over a low-cut frilly white blouse and a skull belt. A white petticoat peaked from beneath the slit of her black miniskirt.

"Child, I am beyond devastated to see you on a day like this looking like that. You are not even masked. And where are your beads? 'Cause I know you've been to the parades."

"I gave them all away."

"I can't fix that, but we gotta fix this," she said, pointing to my outfit.

And with that she began to disrobe in the middle of the street, which wasn't that big of a deal, especially not in the Quarter on Fat Tuesday. Luckily, underneath her pirate wench costume, she wore a sequined thong and pasties over a full body suit.

The tricky part was dressing me. I don't know how she did it, but like a magician, she managed to throw her costume over my jeans and take off my clothes underneath with a minimum of exposure to the crowd. Her miniskirt hit me about mid-calf, and she was able to cinch in the waist of the corset to fit my own. In about five minutes flat, she transformed me into a sexy pirate wench. The only issue was the oversized lacy blouse, which fell off my shoulders, exposing not only too much skin but half my bra. Prepared for any costume malfunction, she reached into the v-front of her thong and pulled out a safety pin. Like a costume designer from *Project Runway* working under pressure, she gathered up the extra fabric and pinned it together in back.

"It's Mardi Gras, baby. Don't cover up those boobies," a man shouted from behind her.

I recognized his raspy voice. Without a doubt, the one person in the world I did not want to see had seen me.

"Which one of you sleazebags are trash-talking to my girl?" Miz Cocktail whipped around, prepared to slap the snot out of the offender.

I searched the crowd. I thought I saw a flash of a Resident Evil cap, but I couldn't be sure. The man wearing it disappeared into the crowd.

"Whoever it was, I think he's gone," I said.

"Okay then, let's see how you look."

Miz Cocktail turned me around so I could see my own reflection in an oval mirror in the bay window of an antique store.

"You look too fabulous to be left alone on the streets. Would you like Miz Cocktail to be your escort for the rest of the evening?"

The back pocket of the jeans I was holding beeped. I reached in, retrieved my cell, and read the text.

"Oh, thanks for the offer. But I'll be okay. Better than okay," I said. "But do you mind taking my street clothes back to the bar?"

"Sure, honey, but what's going on?"

I smiled. Lewis had sent me a message.

Beano wants you to meet him on the steps of St. Mary's.

There it was. My prayers had been answered. The rest was up to the power of my love and the machinations of my voodoo queen.

19.

I walked briskly through the Quarter. Over on Bourbon Street, tourists continued to swill Pat O'Brien hurricanes like lemonade in summer. But for the true families of New Orleans, the day was wrapping up, the parades finished, the house parties winding down. Because when folks start carousing at seven in the morning, they are tuckered out by sundown. The evening had turned chilly; I quickened my pace as I turned on Chartres not because I was cold but because I felt unsettled. The deeper I got into the neighborhood, the emptier the streets became. For some reason, the quietness bothered me. Once again, I felt eyes on me, like someone watching from behind one of the shuttered windows of the row houses that lined the street. Yet those windows were closed tight, braced against the night. I stopped. Listened. Glanced over my shoulder. I was alone.

I walked past the Old Ursuline Convent's French Colonial façade and crossed the street to St. Mary's chapel. A single set of steps led to gray wooden doors with golden crosses. I stood out front, shifting my weight from foot to foot, as I waited.

Every building in New Orleans has a story to tell and the story of the Old Ursuline Convent, the oldest building in the Mississippi Valley, was one of survival. Three hundred years ago, the sisters of Ursula braved pirates and disease to settle in the mud hole that was New Orleans, the city barely ten years old at the time. Maybe that's why Beano wanted to meet at St. Mary's. Maybe he was saying that whatever happened, we would survive this too.

I heard someone approaching from the east—the click of

what sounded like heels on uneven pavement. I turned and I couldn't believe what I saw. There was M— striding toward me.

I whipped out my cell and texted Lewis with a succinct *WTF?*

He texted back immediately. *Beano says it's time for you to make peace with her.*

M— was not masked; she wore expensive, frayed jeans and high-heeled boots. If she had begun the day with make-up, it was long gone. But her beauty was uncompromised. My heart sunk. If Antwone were to appear, the last person I wanted to be standing next to was M—.

"I don't know what's going on, but you have to leave. I came here to see Beano, not you," I said.

"No, you came to see Antwone."

So Beano had told her.

Frustrated, I slapped my fist against the chapel door.

"Don't be mad at Beano," she said. "When he ran into me in the Treme, I was a mess. I don't know why, but I just broke down when I came across a tribe of Mardi Gras Indians. You knew Antwone's granddaddy had been a Big Chief, right?"

Well, of course I did. I had ridden beside his headdress when we evacuated New Orleans. But I didn't share any of that with her. I just nodded so she could finish her story.

"Watching them chant and dance just did me in. It was like losing him all over again."

I tried to steel myself against her sad story, because I did not want to admit that we had anything in common, including losing the one we both loved.

"What breaks my heart is that he never knew that I planned to forgive him all along. I had every intention of getting back together."

"I think he knew," I said, aware of the proof I wore around my neck, the fleur-de-lis he had bought for her.

"I was wrong about Antwone. I accused him of being a player, when all along he was a hero," she said, holding back tears.

I thought about pointing out that the two were not mutually exclusive but decided against it.

"I understand now how all the things that made me crazy, all those other girls, didn't mean anything. He was just trying to figure out who he was. Who he was gonna be."

"But not all boys act the way he did, say they love one and mess around with another," I said.

"If all boys were as good-looking and smooth-talking as Antwone, maybe they would. Just because they could."

"Look, I don't want to talk about *him* with you. I'm sorry you had a bad day, but so did I. Maybe we should just leave it at that."

"I'll go, if you promise to do something for me," she said.

I hesitated; I didn't want to get trapped in the game of making promises I couldn't keep. Still it was getting late, and I didn't know how much time I had. I was afraid that just like Cinderella, my brand of voodoo magic expired at midnight.

"What do you want me to do?"

"The last time I was with Antwone, right before the storm, I said terrible things to him."

I knew only too well; I had heard it all from my bedroom window.

"If you see him again, please tell him I take it all back. I do love him. I went off on him because I was scared of losing him."

"Those other girls didn't mean anything. You said so yourself," I argued.

"I wasn't worried about those other girls. I was afraid of losing him to you."

My entire high school career had been spent living in the shadow of this ideal woman, this object of everyone's affection and envy. To think she had looked beyond her narcissistic self to consider me a threat was unimaginable. And yet there we were, facing each other as equals. I considered carefully before asking: "Did my being white have anything to do with it?"

She laughed out loud. "Why do you white girls want to remove color from the conversation? Ask any Black woman I know, and she'll tell you that you're being white has everything to do with everything, Camille."

I thought about telling her about my great-grandfather but decided against it. I realized that my having Black blood did not give me the right to claim the legacy or the race, because I had grown up with the privilege that comes with being white. To pretend otherwise would be a lie.

I studied her face in a new light and I saw a reflection of my own pain. Before, I failed to notice what should have been apparent. Like me, she had lost him to the storm. And like me, she had not recovered. And the truth was perhaps we never would. Maybe you never get over losing someone you love to violence—whether it's a stray bullet or a terrible car crash or a stranger's knife or the waters of a treacherous hurricane. Maybe you never recover from that kind of death, the kind that comes without warning to someone so young. Maybe that kind of death leaves a hole in your heart forever.

Moved, I unclasped the fleur-de-lis pendant—the one I swore I would never take off—and gave it to her.

"It's beautiful," she said quietly.

"He bought it for you. And even after he told me so, I couldn't bring myself to part with it. He loved you. He loves you still."

She fastened the clasp around her neck; the charm rested perfectly against her skin. The animosity between us fading, I started to go in for a hug but thought better of it.

Before leaving, she said, "Thank you for giving the necklace to me. I mean that. It's not easy to let go of what little pieces of him we have left."

After the click of her high-heeled boots began to fade, I sunk down on the steps of St. Mary's, trying to make sense of what had become of my life.

I startled when I heard the heavy wooden doors of the chapel creak open. Just as I turned to see who it was, a man lunged from the inside of the candlelit narthex, a glimmer of silver in his hand.

Before I could scream, McGee grabbed me, twisted my arm behind my back, and dragged me into the chapel. The massive wooden doors slammed behind us.

I had been right. The hat I'd seen on Royal was his; the eyes I'd felt on me as I walked the neighborhood were his. He had followed me through the Quarter and when he saw me stop at the steps of St. Mary's, he climbed over the convent wall, jimmied open a side door with his knife, and entered the silent, empty chapel. Through the cracks in the uneven doors, McGee had listened to my conversation with M— and waited patiently for her to leave.

His attack in full force, he dragged me down the aisle toward the altar at knifepoint. As red votive candles, symbols of the Eucharist, danced in the darkness, he whispered in my ear, "I've never done anybody in a church before. How about you? You ever make out with some young buck in the back pew, hoping the priest wouldn't see? Or sneak into the chapel after school and let some boy fumble with his cock, put it inside you?"

An involuntary moan emitted from somewhere deep inside me. He took a step back and turned me around so that he could see my face. He kept the knife at my throat.

"No, you never done it in a church, good little Catholic girl like you. You never done it at all, have you? Oh my, that's gonna make it all the sweeter for me, taking a virgin in this holy place. Why, it's practically scriptural."

I choked back tears; I didn't want to give him the satisfaction of seeing how scared I was.

"Ever since I saw you at your daddy's bar, I could see you had a thing for me. Now I'm just gonna give you what you've wanted all along. A little piece of me in you."

"You got that all wrong."

"I know how you girls are. You say no, but what you really want is a man like me to make you do the dirty, secret little things you only dreamed about."

I began to cry. I couldn't help myself.

"There, there, boo," he said, wiping my tears away with the

blade of his knife. "You aren't my first, don't you know, and you certainly won't be my last. But you just might turn out to be my best."

Even though I was scared to death, I knew if I were to survive, I had to be bold.

"If that's the way it's gonna be, then put away that knife and do me like a real man."

My words had the desired effect; they gave him pause. His grip on me relaxed, and he pulled the knife away. I took advantage of his moment of hesitation and kneed him hard in the groin. He yelped like a whipped dog. The knife skittered across the floor, the handle facing me. We both dove for it. He was bigger than me, but I was neither drunk nor stupid. I got to it first and stood up, armed with his knife, the one that had once belonged to me.

He lumbered to his feet, and when he saw me holding the blade, he faltered, weighing my commitment. He took a tentative step toward me. Then another. But I stayed my ground.

"My daddy always said wasn't nothing to killing someone with a gun. Son-of-a-bitch knew firsthand what he was talking about. He'd done time when I was little for blowing the face right off his girlfriend with a twelve-gauge shotgun. I watched him do it from across the room. When he got out of prison, we moved to Bayou Cocodrie. I begged him to buy me a rifle, but he refused, probably because he was afraid I'd turn on him some night and blow his useless ass right off the planet. But when I turned fifteen, he gave me that knife instead and warned me not to get into a fight until I was ready to watch someone die. Up close and personal-like. He said a knife fight was a messy, bloody business, and he didn't think my pansy-ass was ready. He said I hadn't developed an appetite for killing yet."

I flinched; McGee saw. His smile widened.

"Turned out my daddy was dead wrong," he said, laughing at his own bad joke. "I did him in that very night. Dumped him in the swamp afterward. Nobody ever knew. More like nobody even cared. What about you, boo? You got the stomach for killing?"

Deciding that I did not, he lunged at me.

I slashed the blade through the air, aiming for his throat. But the knife missed its mark. Instead I sliced open his face, from his ear down to his chin. The cut was deep, oozing crimson onto the floor. With a stab straight to his heart and a twist of the blade, I could kill him easy and watch him bleed out on the chapel floor.

If you had told me at that moment how the night would end, I would not have believed you. My own memories are clouded, so I must trust the tainted recollections of the others who survived. Because there were others, a collision of forces that would come together with deadly consequences. So what follows now is the narrative I have pieced together from their stories and mine.

My story up to this point you know already.

But the second story involves a float builder from Slidell: forty-three-year-old Gerald Hoskins, who was driving a huge tractor-drawn float down Rampart, headed for a warehouse by the river. Recently married for the first time, Gerald worked for the biggest float building company in New Orleans. He had designed the float he drove that night, a one-story affair that could hold thirty revelers. On the front was a magnificently terrifying Medusa, who had hair of purple serpents, animated to coil and recoil with menace.

But Gerald's true pride was not in the artistry of the float but in the structure that supported it. The winged Gorgon's frame was double the size of most floats. It had eight wheels with huge steel rims to support the weight of the throws and people piled on the float.

"Folks have no idea what it takes to drive a fifty-ton float down the street. They just want the beads. That's really what the season is about," Gerald told his new wife, barely married a year at the time. "It's all about the beads."

"Then why don't you do something else for a living?" his wife asked. Lisette was expecting their first child and she was tired of his long work hours.

Gerald melted under the gaze of her sweet brown eyes and promised to quit his float-building job and go to work for her daddy's big construction company instead.

And then Katrina hit. And he broke his promise.

"We've all been through so much. We need us some Mardi Gras. I have to see it through one more season."

"I oughta make you put that in writing," Lisette said, pretending to be miffed. But deep down inside, she loved the city as much as he. Why, they even held their wedding outdoors in Louis Armstrong Park where they pledged their love and loyalty not only to each other, but also to Dr. John, to the Saints, and to the Crescent City itself.

As he pulled his Medusa toward the Den of Muses, half an hour away from parking the float and leaving the job for good, he wondered how much he would miss it.

A few blocks away, the third story was unfolding. Beano's three-year-old half-brother, Kemper, was walking home from the parades with his dad, Langley, and his grandma, Roselle, who was thrilled that her daughter-in-law had stayed behind in Boston.

Kemper loved watching parades and catching beads. Being small gave him a distinct advantage. While adults struggled to catch the beads in the air as they were thrown, he kept his eye to the ground and grabbed up the baubles that slipped through their grip. He scored big on Fat Tuesday; he had so many throws around his neck that he waddled when he walked. His dad picked him up to carry him back home, but he didn't like that one bit.

"Put me down, Daddy," he cried for the fourth time.

Exhausted by the crowds and looking forward to a short shower and a long drink at his mother's house, Langley hesitated. But Roselle, as she often did, took the little boy's side.

"Oh, honey, don't let's fight. Let Kemper walk. We only have a few blocks to go. What's the harm?"

Langley put off that well-deserved bourbon and prepared to let his son walk the rest of the way home.

Back in the chapel at St. Mary's, McGee's life hung in the balance. One twist of the blade and it would be over. But it turned out McGee was right. When push came to shove, I couldn't do it. I didn't have the stomach for killing. Instead, I threw the knife over his head, far away from the both of us, toward the gilded altar of the church. I bolted toward the door, certain he would go for the knife and that the time it would take to retrieve it would give me a head start.

And while I grabbed the handle of the heavy church doors, not too far away, Gerald was making a sweeping right turn from North Rampart onto Esplanade. As he drove through a canopy of trees on the street where Roselle lived, one of the serpents on Medusa's head caught a limb and snagged a hidden power line.

Four blocks away, the lights flickered off and Langley exclaimed, "Oh hell, what now?"

"Welcome to life after the storm," Roselle said. "Power comes and power goes. Everybody's off grid."

SLAM! The doors of the chapel shut behind me. But once again, I had miscalculated. McGee didn't go for the knife; he came after me. Startled, I tripped on the uneven steps of St. Mary's and tumbled to the ground. He leaned over me; his blood dripped on my starched white petticoat. I screamed out Antwone's name.

What I did not know at the time was that his host body was only minutes away, the final player in our collective story. Beano strolled down the dark street, hand in hand with Lewis, toward his grandmother's rambling mansion. He knew his father was in town for Mardi Gras, and he wanted to see Kemper, but most of all, he wanted to prove to Lewis that he loved him by bringing him home to meet the family.

Meanwhile, Gerald decided to keep driving. Nothing he could do about a downed power line that could take hours to fix. So instead, he flipped the switch on the fiber optic lights, hoping to use Medusa's snake hair to light his way back to the Den of Muses. But nothing happened. The float rolled to a stop. He fiddled with the loose wires in the dark.

Back on the chapel steps, I was on my own. McGee yanked me to my feet. With a surge of adrenalin, I broke free and took off running, heading for Esplanade. McGee followed close behind. I raced past houses with brightly colored shutters that now appeared grim, down the endless block of menacing balconies towering over me.

While I ran for my life, Beano met up with his family just outside the iron fence to Roselle's mansion. It was a warm reunion with hugs and kisses all around. Kemper wrapped his chubby little arms around his big brother's leg. Langley held his hand out to Lewis.

"I don't believe we've had the pleasure."

Beano threw his arm around Lewis's shoulder and announced proudly, "Daddy, I want you to meet my boyfriend, Lewis Sinclair."

Langley withdrew his hand of welcome. Roselle finally broke the awkward silence. "And here I thought the reason you came home was to see me," she said slyly. "But now that I've met your handsome young man, I think I know the real reason you decided to come back to New Orleans."

"I think that's enough," Langley cautioned. He preferred his son's homosexuality to remain closeted, in deference to his wife.

Suddenly, Medusa's coiled snake hair came alive, lighting a narrow path on the dark street. As the float rolled toward them, a stream of water from an ice chest emptied earlier glistened in the green-cast flow of Medusa's serpent locks. And in that man-made stream was a strand of purple acorn-shaped beads, shiny and bright.

A sense of wonder fell over the family as the snakes on

Medusa's horrifying head uncoiled, reaching out into the night. And while they looked up, Kemper looked down to the beads in the street. And in that split second with the adults' attention elsewhere, Kemper broke free and ran toward the glittery throws.

I hit the intersection of Chatres and Esplanade a split second before the float. I didn't see Kemper, not at first. What I do remember is spotting his family. I ran into the street toward the safe haven promised by the presence of others.

Gerald never saw the child who was bending over to pick up discarded beads. But he did see me, a crazed young pirate's wench, flying across the street. He swerved to avoid hitting me and in doing so headed straight for the little boy who was in the direct path of the tractor float. McGee caught up to me, grabbed my arm, and stopped me cold.

From across the street, the young man turned and I saw Beano's face for the first time. In the play of shadows, I saw what only I could see—the sudden appearance of Antwone. My boyfriend took over my best friend's body and sprang into action. He darted into the street, jerked Kemper up, and pushed him toward the sidewalk and out of the path of the float.

He looked up just as the float barreled over him. He hurdled over the front of the tractor, catapulting over the grill. Gerald yanked up the emergency brake just as Antwone slammed into the face of Medusa head-on. Antwone crumpled and his body slid underneath the float.

I saw it all in slow motion. His body flying through the air. The collision with Medusa. Streaks of his blood running down her face. I could hear the horrific bone-crushing sound of his body as the massive front wheels of the float rolled over him.

McGee held tight to my arm. We watched the whole, horrible thing like tourists on Bourbon Street.

"Shit, boo, we gotta get out of here," McGee said. "Nothing we can do. That boy's dead."

From where we stood, I could see a stream of blood creeping

across the pavement, mixing with the river of water. I knew that McGee was right, that the body trapped underneath the tractor had no life. But I didn't care. I looked deep into the eyes of the monster that gripped my arm—this rapist, this daddy-killer—and begged him to show one ounce of humanity.

"We have to try."

McGee sighed and I broke free and ran to the other side of the float where Langley and Lewis were trying to pull his body out from under the float. I don't know why McGee didn't just get the hell out of there. But he didn't; he joined me and the others.

"Beano's leg is trapped under the wheel," Lewis cried, panicked.

Because I was the smallest, I dropped to the ground and slid under the float to see what could be done.

"You gotta pull the tractor forward to free him," I screamed, sliding back out from under the float.

"That boy is dead," McGee repeated. "Look at all that blood."

"Half of it's yours," I snapped. And truthfully, the gash from his face continued to bleed, mixing with the river on the ground.

The two older men looked at him for the first time, then back at me. They didn't know how we fit into this horrible mess, but like when the levees gave way and the water came, there was no time for questions.

"I called 911. Maybe we should wait until they get here," Roselle said, cradling the sobbing Kemper in her arms.

"We don't have time," Langley said. "He's bleeding out."

Looking back, trying to free him from underneath the tractor was probably the worst idea ever. But since the storm, we no longer blindly trusted that help would arrive in time, if at all.

"Once I pull forward, the float may roll back before the engine engages. I could end up running over him a second time," Gerald said.

"What if we throw our weight on the float while you pull the tractor forward?" I suggested.

"You got any idea how much this baby weighs? We need ten, twenty men at least," Gerald said.

"Well, you got three. So just do what the little lady says," McGee said, narrowing his eyes at me. I had the unshakeable feeling that he planned on making me pay for his magnanimity later.

Gerald shook his head and climbed on the tractor. Langley, Lewis, and McGee rammed their bodies against the bar rising up out of the axel over the wheel. On the count of three, the men threw themselves against the float, straining under the load, summoning up superhuman strength. Gerald turned the engine over, but instead of rolling backwards, the tractor-drawn float lurched forward. In that split-second, I pulled his bloodied body out from under the float and into my arms.

"I got him," I yelled.

Gerald yanked up the emergency brake, but as he did, the float rolled backwards as he first predicted. The sudden surge caught all three men off guard. As the float bore down, Lewis leapt out of harm's way; Langley stumbled over to the curb. But McGee lost his footing. He slipped in the murky river of water and blood and was sucked under the float. We watched helplessly as the mighty Medusa rolled over his body and crushed his head. He didn't scream out for help; he didn't make a sound at all. The driver didn't even realize what had happened until he jumped off the tractor and saw McGee's brains oozing out from under the float.

I don't believe in grace or salvation or redemption. Not anymore. Not after what we've been through. But I do believe that in the last seconds of his life, McGee rose above his worthless self to do one good thing, his life traded for another.

"Oh lord, I've gone and killed two men tonight," Gerald cried out, racked with guilt.

Lewis was the one who noticed first. "He's breathing. Oh my god, Beano's still breathing."

Sure enough, I could see it, too—the rise and fall of his chest, the raspy gasp for oxygen. But I was the only one who knew that it was Antwone, not Beano who possessed the broken body I held in my arms. Gerald left to grab a small first aid kit from underneath the tractor seat, as if Band-Aids and alcohol wipes were of any use at all.

I cried out to the spirit of Marie Laveau, "What have we done? What have we done?"

A grey, swirling mist rose from the open grate on the side of the road, enveloping the two of us in watery magic. Inside the smoky fog, I heard her voice.

Let the healing power begin. Let the Earth be whole again. The Earth is my mother and I am her child. The Earth is my lover. Free and wild. Heal on the outside; heal within. Land and sea, fire and wind. With love, sincere, I chant his prayer. To make mankind begin to care. Let every sister and every brother. Heal the wounds.

With Marie Laveau's ritual chant pulsing through my body, I leaned in close to Antwone and kept my promise, whispering that M— had never stopped loving him, that she loved him still and that so did I.

Antwone's eyes fluttered open and the swirling mist was sucked back into the world beneath the grate. And in that split second, he left. In his place, Beano cried out. His back arched. His eyes rolled back into his head. His body seized in a wave after wave of violent contractions that lasted two minutes at least. When it was over, he turned away from me and threw up yellow bile on the pavement. It took him a moment to get his bearings and then the first thing he did was ask about Kemper.

"He's a little scraped up from skidding across the rough pavement, but he's okay," I answered.

Dazed, he sat up, dusted himself off like a rodeo rider who had taken a tumble off a horse.

"Help me up," he said, holding out a hand.

We were all beyond shocked, no one more than his father who tried to stop him.

"You shouldn't move until the paramedics get here. Your leg could be broken."

"I'm a little shook up. That's all."

I looked down and saw that his gaping wound had healed, as had the scrapes on his face. His pants and shirt were torn and stained with blood, but the gashes were gone. There was not a mark on him.

"Praise the lord," Roselle exclaimed. "If ever there were a miracle, this sure as hell is it!"

Gerald sunk to the curb, his head in his hands, and mumbled nonsensically how he had killed two men, only to see one resurrected, like Jesus on the cross.

He sounded crazy.

It was crazy.

Roselle's jubilation quickly shifted into deep concern. If there were one thing Roselle wanted no part of, it was "crazy." She was one of those women who believed your name should only be mentioned in the press three times: when you were born, when you got married, and when you died.

"What on earth are we gonna say when the police get here? How are we going to explain all of this?" Roselle asked.

"We have to tell the truth, tell them what happened," Langley said.

"I think not," Roselle replied emphatically.

Langley backed down. He knew better than to argue with his mother, a battle he was sure to lose. His wife had the ability to suck the oxygen out of the room; his mother could suck it out of the city. After a brief conversation, it was clear that not one of us wanted to get tangled up in a lengthy police investigation, especially Gerald. And besides, who in the world would believe us?

I recognized the necessity for a united plan. The first thing was to remove Kemper from the scene of the many crimes. He had seen and heard too much already. I instructed Beano and Lewis to take the little boy into the house and to stay put. There was no reason for any of them to be a part of the story I was already spinning.

Langley stopped Beano as he opened the gate. He embraced his son and threw a welcoming arm around Lewis's shoulder and said he was sorry and that he loved him. Although his apology was sweet as pie, we didn't have time for dessert. I broke it up, got the three boys into the house, and turned back to business. In the ten minutes before the police arrived, we concocted the following version of events.

McGee tried to rape me.

I escaped.

He pursued.

Chasing me, he ran across the dark intersection, where he slipped and fell in the water. Gerald swerved to avoid hitting me and, in doing so, the wheels of the float ran over McGee. He was crushed under the weight of Medusa.

Three eyewitnesses, Langley, Roselle, and myself, swore it was an accident, that the float driver never saw the victim. Later the lab would confirm the blood on my petticoat belonged to McGee and the knife would be recovered in the chapel of St. Mary's.

After I explained how McGee had stalked me and described his past crimes, the chief investigator on the scene turned to Gerald and said, "Sounds like you did the world a favor."

And that was that.

They bought the lie like it was truth.

Beano watched the whole affair from an upstairs window, Lewis at his side. I could see his profile lit by candles through the branches of the sycamore in the front yard. He never took his eyes off me.

They say that the eyes are the windows to your soul, which perhaps explains how I knew that it was not his eyes that were watching me. They belonged to Antwone.

20.

I f there is a lesson to be learned from your dying, then what
is it?"

That was the question I asked Antwone as we soaked in
the waters of Gina's claw-footed tub.

"Maybe there isn't one," he replied as he cupped warm water
with his hand and dribbled it along my arm.

An hour earlier, we had left Roselle's gated mansion. Beano's
family was confused. They wanted to know where he was going
this late at night and why he was leaving with me. Only Lewis
had an inkling as to what had truly happened at that fateful
intersection, and after witnessing a life taken and a life saved, he
gave his blessing to our being together one last time.

We hailed a cab, but our bloodstained clothes put off the driver. He didn't want his brand new upholstery getting all bloody.
He offered to call an ambulance, but after we convinced him
that the blood was dry and not our own, he agreed to give us
a ride to the Garden District. It didn't hurt that we paid twice
the fare.

We rode in silence and when we pulled up into the empty
oak-lined driveway, Gina was waiting at the door. Like Lewis,
she trusted that what I told them both was true—that by daybreak, life as we once had known it would return.

She closed the heavy oak door and pulled me aside, leaving
Antwone alone by the stairs. Although she didn't understand
the magic, she moved quickly from the supernatural to the
practical.

"Are you planning on having sex?" Gina asked.

"Yes," I answered, deciding for myself at that moment.

"Do you think that's a good idea?" Gina asked.

"Define *good idea*," I said.

"Oh hell," Gina said, giving in without a fuss. "The candles are in the top shelf of the armoire, and the condoms are in the top left-hand drawer of the dresser, underneath the bras. Promise me that you'll use one 'cause whatever is going on, you still need protection."

"I promise," I said, sealing the deal with a heartfelt hug.

As he and I walked up the stairs to her suite, Gina retired to one of the guest bedrooms. Before turning down the hall, she cautioned us to lock the door, just in case tomorrow was the first Ash Wednesday ever that The Betsy stirred before evening Mass.

We stepped into Gina's room and he locked the door as instructed. Antwone wanted to clean up, and I, too, felt the need to wash away the evening. I showed him the bathroom, the claw-foot tub, big enough for two. He stripped off his clothes, letting them drop to the floor as I drew the bath, the dark bathroom lit by one candle. I couldn't help but stare at how beautiful he was. In the candlelight, he looked like a bronzed Atlas capable of taking on the weight of the world. Once again I wondered how the waters could have taken someone so young, so strong, so physically perfect. He slid into the bath and closed his eyes. When he opened them, I hadn't moved, not one muscle.

"Are you coming in?" he asked.

"Yeah," I said, suddenly shy. It wasn't just that I didn't want him analyzing my body the way I had his. It was more than that. Scarier than that. I felt vulnerable and not in a good way, like I was dirty, like something deep down inside of me had been spoiled forever. I could still feel the breath of another on my neck and the blade of his knife at my throat. His whispered threats ran through my head. McGee was like a bad dream that stays with you even after you wake up.

Antwone rested his eyes, sinking deeper into the tub. I undressed quickly, throwing off my clothes, adding to the pile of his. All jumbled together on the tile floor, the clothes reminded me of the mess Katrina made of our belongings in what used to be my backyard. I stepped into the tub and slid into the water. Even though I knew the water would transform my straight hair into a frizzy mess when it dried, I dunked my head under, fully immersing myself. I needed the baptism of waters to erase the memory of McGee.

As we soaked in the tub, I tried to make sense of what had happened to us.

"Was it voodoo magic or my cry for help that called you home?"

"I don't think it matters."

"Don't you want to know what it all means?" I asked.

"Sometimes things happen and you never understand the why. Preachers promise that we will find the answers to life on Earth in the next one. But maybe they got it wrong. My dying felt very non-denominational, and when I finally leave this place to wherever it is I'm going, maybe the questions won't matter anymore."

"If even death doesn't give us answers to the most basic of our questions, then what is the point to any of our stories?"

"The point is that your life will go on and mine will not," he said as he pulled me to him. With my back leaning against his chest, he wrapped his arms around me and told me about my life in his honey-laced voice.

"You'll finish high school and go on to college—not here, though, but on the East Coast. In Boston. I hear they have a couple of good schools up there," he said with just the right amount of irony. Two of them, BU and Harvard, had recruited him hard to play football.

"They'll be nobody else like you in Beantown. And your freshman year, you'll have a roommate that makes you crazy in a bad way, but your sophomore year, you'll meet a boy who makes you crazy in a good way. I'm serious. That's the way it's gonna be. My baby girl's gonna break some hearts—two or three, at least. And someone will break yours."

"Somebody already has," I said, interrupting.

"Hush. I'm telling you your life. Where was I? Oh yeah. You'll change majors at least four times but decide on creative writing. And you'll come back home after graduation and get a job at a start-up Internet company that hosts travel blogs. And even though you'll leave New Orleans from time to time, you'll never stay away long. And you'll get married before you turn thirty. Your first husband will be a man of color, and you'll have two kids. Your second husband will be white and you'll have two more kids."

"Four kids?" I said, laughing. "I'm not even sure I want one."

"Like I said, you'll have four babies with skin of different colors. But all of them—white and Black—will have beautiful nappy hair, just like their mother. And while they're growing up, you'll work part time. First, writing copy at an ad agency and later for the Louisiana Film Commission. And after your daddy dies and your last little girl grows up and goes off to college, you and your mother will run the Cock's Comb. She'll do the books, but you'll be the one behind the bar, serving up drinks and stories."

I interrupted. "Are you making this up for fun? Or has dying given you some special power of prophesy?"

"For such a small girl, you sure ask a lot of big questions. You wanna know how it ends or not?"

"Of course, I wanna know."

"Anyway, around the Quarter, you'll be known as the 'the teller of tales.' Every night you'll entertain the regulars and the tourists at the bar with stories of the city you love and the people who love it back. But only after you bury your mother—only then will you tell mine. The years will come and they will go. You will outlive both husbands, one child, and most of your friends. And you will grow old and soft and wrinkled."

"And you will always be young. You will be forever the boy I loved," I said and began to cry.

He dried my tears and then my body as we stepped out of the tub. Afterwards, he wrapped me in one of Gina's fluffy towels.

Still flushed from the warm waters, we left the bath for the bed, dropped our towels, and slid under the sheets.

We took it real slow as if we had all the time in the world. Lying side by side, facing each other, our bodies close, but not touching. With barely a breath between us, he showered me with long, sweet kisses.

He propped himself up on an elbow and admired my naked breasts. "You have beautiful titties, baby girl," he said.

I blushed. "I always thought they were too small."

"More than a mouthful's just a waste of skin," he said, smiling. And to prove his point, he lowered himself toward me and cupped my breast into his mouth, flicking his tongue across my nipple. He rose up, took me in his arms, and kissed me, long and hard. This time, I did not close my eyes. I was afraid if I did, I would lose him again, like before. He pushed his fingers inside of me, gently massaging me from inside out. I arched my back, moaning in ecstasy. He whispered in my ear, urging me to let go, to give in, to come.

But I resisted. I wanted more than just his fingers inside of me. I wanted him. All of him.

Remembering my promise to Gina, I pulled away, slipped out of the bed, and started for the dresser, and that was when he noticed the ink on the small of my back.

"Girl, what have you gone and done? You got a tramp stamp bobcat on your butt."

"I did it for you. *A* is for Antwone," I said, grabbing one of the condoms buried under the bras.

He smiled and shook his head. "That's a lot of responsibility to lay on a man."

When I came back to bed, he noticed what I held in my hand.

"We don't need a condom," he said, pulling me back toward him.

His reaction threw me for a loop. I was in love, for sure, but I was not stupid.

"Well, I'd be more comfortable if we used one."

"What I meant," he said, wrapping his arm around my waist, "is that we won't need one because we're not going to have sex."

"Why not?" I asked. I knew he wanted me.

"Oh, baby girl, you're going to have a hard-enough time getting over me. But if I sleep with you, I'd ruin you for anybody else," he said, laughing.

His lashes brushed across my cheek in a butterfly kiss.

"You think you're that good?" I asked, challenging him.

"I *know* I'm that good," he said, outlining my breast with his fingertip. "But I saw how you undressed. How you didn't want me watching you. Why you think that is?"

"I'm not sure," I said.

"I think it's because of what he almost did to you."

I knew he was right, but I believed that making love to him would cleanse the bad juju that coursed through my body like blood.

"It'll take time for you to get over what happened tonight," he said quietly.

"But the one thing we don't have is time," I argued.

"If we make love, the good and the bad will get all mixed up together and mess you up real bad. Trust me to do what's right for both of us, baby girl."

And so I did, because I didn't know what else to do. I let him take me into his arms. I relaxed under his touch. And as he began kissing me all over my body, I felt myself slipping away. I cannot adequately describe what happened next. Together we left the bedroom and went down to the river. Walking side by side, wading knee-deep into the canal, I felt like myself and not myself. We were in the river, water churning around us, touching me everywhere, caressing my body. My thighs wet with him. Wet with water. Skin next to skin. Intertwined together. Dancing in the wake of powerful urges. I was filled with a need so great it longed for release. And yet I refused to let go. I would not give in to climax. I knew if I did, the feeling would go away and I could not bear that possibility. I resisted release and chose instead to teeter on the precipice of deep desire. Wanting it. Wanting him. Spinning higher and higher. Out of control.

And as our bodies swirled in the waters, it was as if I could listen in on the private conversations in the heart of others— conversations that knew no color or earthly boundary. I heard things he wished he had said to M— and what he wanted to say to me. I heard their love story as I listened to my own. The stories spun in my head like an old radio program all the time he was kissing me as the river lapped up against our legs. He loved her; he loved me. He loved us both. Our stories were all twisted together like our clothes on the bathroom floor, like the wreckage of our homes after the storm. I realized that the boy I had fallen in love with, the one who lived next door to me, was an apparition, a ghost of my own making. But when his soul took flight and his spirit entered the body of another, I discovered his true nature, the man he was, and a glimpse into the man he would have become. As we danced in the waters, I saw the truth of what he had been trying to tell me all along, that I needed to release the past and move us all forward to the place where we needed to be. And then, suddenly, I remembered no more.

I resurfaced from my imagined watery deep and came into full consciousness with a start.

Antwone reached over and gently tugged on one of the corkscrew curls forming as my hair dried.

"Girl, you got a Mardi Gras going on every day on top of your head."

He pulled his hand away, looked at me with gentle eyes, and said simply, "It's time."

I knew he was leaving me. But this time I did not blink or look away. I watched his skin turn from coffee and cream to freckled white. His features slowly morphed from his own to that of my best friend. When the physical transformation was complete, his essence floated above Beano's sleeping body, like fog lifting on the riverbank. And then he was gone.

A hard winter chill swept over me. I slipped out of bed and into Gina's long fleece robe. I covered up Beano with a quilted comforter and let him sleep.

I kept watch with my silent tears until he woke.

☙

"Do you know the purpose of the lively music that dances us out of the cemetery and into the streets?" Aisha asked as she trimmed my hair the morning of Antwone's funeral.

Three days into Lent, the remains of a young man were found upriver, buried in mud and debris. At first, they thought it was a homicide case, but some detective had the wherewithal to check the dental records on file of those still missing from the storm. A DNA sample from a lock of his baby hair confirmed that the remains belonged to Antwone. So Bama had what she'd been waiting for—a body to bury.

I considered for a moment before I answered Aisha's question. It felt like a test.

"I'd say it's because a person can only listen to sad songs for so long, like a reminder that you can't live in grief forever," I said, proud of my answer.

But it only took about two seconds for Aisha to shut me down and set me straight.

"It has nothing to do with us. It has to do with them. The music is intended to help the newly departed find their way to heaven—to celebrate the final release from life. It, too, is part of the African Diaspora. The call and response, the chanting, the drums, and even the tambourines crossed the seas from Africa with the captive slaves. The music promised freedom, if not from their masters then from the burden of life itself. And so, you see, the music we make now represents not only our loved one's release from this earth, but from the past and from slavery itself."

Aisha continued, "Today, when you bury that precious boy, when the upbeat music begins and it's time to cut his body loose, you must resist the temptation to call him back. I want you to promise me, child, that you will join in the voices of all those who loved him and sing him into heaven."

My daddy told me once that a funeral is more than a declaration that a person has died; it is a testimony that a life has been lived. And that afternoon over five hundred of us gathered in St. Louis Cathedral to honor Antwone's life and to testify that in the short time he had had on earth, he'd touched so many so deeply. None more than me.

After the service, we stepped out of the dark, candlelit cathedral into a sunny winter afternoon. It had rained earlier and puddles of water shimmered with gold in the bright winter sun. Six pallbearers from the football team—Beano among them—carried his white coffin down to the waiting horse-drawn hearse. White horses adorned in purple-flowered wreaths lifted their magnificent heads with an impatient whinny as the pallbearers slid the coffin into the glass-windowed hearse.

As we headed for the cemetery, two limos—carrying Bama, her sister from Lafayette, and those too frail to walk—trailed behind the horse-drawn hearse down the narrow streets of the Quarter. The rest of us promenaded behind the Rebirth Brass Band, which started us off with "Just a Closer Walk with Thee." Bama convinced the band members to forgo their traditional black funeral garb. Instead, they dressed in shades of gold—jackets, shirts, pants, even their suspenders were hues of gold. On their heads they wore deep purple fedoras with golden plumes. At the head of the parade, four men swayed from side to side, dragging one foot to the other in a slow two-step, their right hands over their hearts. Leading us all was a woman, dressed like the men and twirling a matching parasol trimmed in Mardi Gras green.

Hymn after hymn moved us from the funeral service to the burial site. Midway there, we were joined by the Big Chiefs of many of the Mardi Gras Indian tribes, decked out in their feathered finery. The Indian tribes came out in droves to honor the grandson of Big Chief Tito. Among them and in a place of honor was the Spy Boy that Bama befriended. He led us in a call and response so loud that we drowned out the noise spilling from the bars in the Quarter.

The Big Chief say, "He was strong of body and mind."
And the people say, "Lord took him away."
The Big Chief say, "Looked so good, looked so fine."
And the people say, "Lord took him away."
The Big Chief say, "Sacrificed himself for others."
And the people say, "Lord took him away."
The Big Chief say, "Missed by all his sisters and brothers."
And the people say, "Lord took him away."

At the gates of the cemetery, the men in sashes opened the doors of the limo, and Bama and her family joined us on foot. The pallbearers lifted their heavy load and we followed the gleaming white casket through the gates of the city of the dead, greeted by crosses and statues of saints that jutted out at all angles. The band played us to the Despre family crypt and we buried him with music.

After the final prayer by the black-robed priest, the trumpet player hugged Bama and told her, "It's time to say your final goodbyes." She whispered in his ear and he nodded and the band began to play "I'll Fly Away." Right away, the woman leading the band pumped her parasol to the uptown beat and high-step-strutted toward the gates of the cemetery. She wasn't young—she must have been fifty or so—but that old woman could move her feet like a teenage girl. Her shuffling jumps and swaying hips were infectious. The cemetery jolted alive with the sound of singing as the mourners united their voices in song and danced their way into the street.

Some glad morning when this life is o'er/ I'll fly away/ To a home on God's celestial shore/ I'll fly away.

I wanted to be part of that choir of voices, but something held me back. All around me, sadness turned to joy. Women in tight dresses shimmied and shook handkerchiefs in the air. Men jumped and hollered and the somber funeral transformed into an all-out street celebration. But I could not join in.

My head spinning with music, I didn't immediately recognize the beautiful M–, who somehow found me in the crowd.

I'll fly away, fly away, Oh Glory/ I'll fly away (in the morning)/ When I die, Hallelujah, by and by/ I'll fly away.

She'd been crying for sure. A touch of mascara ran down her cheek, forming black teardrops on her perfect skin. She wore a purple dress that hung on her body like second skin. Around her neck was the fleur-de-lis necklace that I had given her on the steps of St. Mary's. But it had been altered. It was no longer whole. Her jeweler had cut it in half and buffed the sharp edges smooth. Without a word, she fastened a second gold chain around my neck. Dangling from that chain was the other half of the necklace that Antwone had bought for her and for her alone. I wear it still. I will wear it forever.

When the shadows of this life have gone/ I'll fly away/ Like a bird from these prison bars has flown/ I'll fly away.

I became part of the single flowing movement of people unified by rhythm—the first line strutting their dance moves while the second liners fell in behind, blowing whistles, hitting cowbells, tapping beer bottles—raising their voices in celebration. Still, I could not join them in song.

The last time I saw him, the night we did not make love, I had been so certain I wanted to have sex with him, but I realized what he had known then—that what I'd needed was a different kind of release, one that would lead to understanding.

Oh, how glad and happy when we meet/ I'll fly away/ No more cold iron shackles on my feet/ I'll fly away.

The priest said he had gone to a better place. But what if he was wrong? Aisha said that the kinder thing to do was to let him go, but what if Antwone was not on the brink of enlightenment but on the precipice of eternal darkness? And what if I could bring him back, how could I not give him one last look at the river he loved? And what if in the process I gave myself one last opportunity to understand the meaning of life itself?

Just a few more weary days and then/ I'll fly away/ To a land where joy shall never end/ I'll fly away.

What if it was something greater than love or voodoo magic that had brought Antwone back from the dead? Had he been allowed to linger to serve some higher purpose? And if so, had this higher purpose now been served? Was it to save a little boy he did not know? Or to rid the world of one evil resident? Or maybe his higher purpose was to be the medium of reconciliation. Beano to his father. The two girls who loved him to each other. Or perhaps it was to reconcile all of us to the tremendous emptiness left behind by his leaving.

At that moment of revelation, Beano caught my eye.

I felt the familiar tug of longing surge within me. Beano saw the look on my face and pleaded with anxious eyes. *Don't do it. Resist. For him. For you. For all of us.* But surprisingly, he didn't run. Instead, he left his lover's protection and made his way through the marchers to me. He took my hands and bowed his head, as if he were surrendering to the power growing inside of me. He was literally leaving the decision in my own hands. If voodoo was involved in the magic I'd witnessed—the visitations from my dead boyfriend—it was long gone, left in the cemetery at the grave of the great queen herself. The ability to call his spirit back resided in me and me alone. I was filled with a sense of powerful calm and I knew deep in my bones that I could do it, sure as I had summoned Beano to my side.

In the past, my resolve to let Antwone go had never been strong enough or lasted long enough. Every time his spirit attempted flight, a selfish desire to possess what could never be mine kept him tethered to earth. I closed my eyes in deep meditative prayer. Seeking wisdom. Asking for strength. My fingertips began to tingle, my body to shudder. But instead of calling him back, I opened my heart and joined in the chorus of mourners.

And I sang him into heaven.

ACKNOWLEDGMENTS

I would also like to thank the two remarkable young women who were the first to read the manuscript and who championed me every step of the way: my daughter, Nancy Shrodes and our friend, Rosanna Xia.